Bonnie J. Cardone

Murder Dives the Caribbean

A Cinnamon Greene Adventure

Mystery

Also by Bonnie J. Cardone

Fiction
Cinnamon Greene Adventure Mysteries
Murder Dives the Caribbean
Murder Dives the Bahamas
The Bride Wore Black

Short Stories
Shark Bait, *Kings River Life*
The Last of the Recycled Cycads, *Last Exit to Murder*
anthology
Murder at the Marietta Inn, *Gone Coastal* anthology

Nonfiction
Fireside Diver
Shipwrecks of Southern California

ISBN: 97809897165-6-7

Published in the United States of America

Sea Scenes
Santa Maria, CA 93455
www.bonniejcardone.com

Dedication

To my children, Pamela and Michael, who have added

immeasurable joy to my life.

MURDER DIVES THE CARIBBEAN

Chapter 1

Our night dive on Bonamer Island's town pier was an underwater photographer's dream, full of interesting creatures. Danny and I had been down more than an hour when he tapped my arm. I reluctantly shifted my attention from a tiny fish to him and he signaled it was time to head back to shore. We were running low on air.

The water was clear and shallow and the moon provided more than enough light to see where we were going. Danny turned off his light and I did the same. We hadn't gone far when the silence was broken by the putt-putt-putt of an outboard engine. It slowed and stopped directly overhead. Surprised, I looked up to see our exhalation bubbles shattering on the bottom of a small boat only 15 feet above us. Moments later, there was a splash as a large object entered the water and plummeted toward us.

Danny and I barely had time to scramble out of the way before the object hit the bottom with a thump, raising a large cloud of sand. We turned on our lights.

As the sand settled and the water cleared, our beams converged on a shocking sight: the body of a man wearing red plaid boxer shorts, a short-sleeved black T-shirt and a scuba diver's black buoyancy vest. The man's mouth and blue eyes were open and his short hair wafted lazily in the water like so much blond seaweed.

The man was anchored to the bottom by a yellow line wrapped around his ankles that was tied to a hook on the top of a concrete cylinder.

The man was dead.

Chapter 2

Holy shit.

The boat sped off.

My first instinct was to get the hell out of there. Danny apparently concurred. It would have been good if we'd had the same direction in mind. Instead, we collided, our flailing fins and bodies creating a sand storm. Visibility dropped to zero.

When we untangled ourselves, Danny consulted his compass and grabbed my hand. My heart pounded and I gulped air through my regulator as we swam rapidly toward shore.

Then my brain began to process what had happened. I work part-time as a forensic photographer for my hometown police department. I've seen dead bodies before. So why was I leaving this one without making a photographic record of it? I shook off Danny's grip. When he turned to look at me, I pointed backward and pantomimed using my camera.

Bubbles burst from Danny's regulator as he shouted "No!" He took hold of my arm and tried to drag me toward shore.

I dug my heels into the bottom and, when Danny lost his grip, headed back. Danny followed, mumbling expletives.

The second sighting of the dead man was just as unsettling as the first. I forced myself to calm down and observe the scene.

While the concrete cylinder that brought the man to the bottom and kept him there looked familiar, I couldn't remember where I'd seen it, or maybe one like it, before.

I motioned Danny to stay put. He uttered more expletives and waggled his finger "no" but settled on the sand as I swam slowly around the body to determine what photos to take and the best places

—

to take them from without disturbing the scene.

I handed my dive light to Danny and indicated that I wanted him to light the scene for me. He wasn't happy about that either but did it anyway. Unfortunately, after my first shot my strobe died. Its battery needed charging. I handed my camera system to Danny and wrestled his video camera from him. I used it until the batteries in its lights died only minutes later.

Danny grabbed my dive computer and checked my air supply before pointing to his computer and then up. He was telling me our scuba tanks were nearly empty and we needed to surface.

Knowing there was a dead guy under me in the dark was spookier than actually seeing him. Now it occurred to me the man might have been murdered and his killers could be nearby. What if they tried to run us down with their boat?

I scanned the ocean around us when we surfaced. Danny did, too. We saw nothing unusual. Danny took coordinates to fix the location of the body before we raced toward shore. I was out of breath and shivering from shock when I reached the sidewalk.

Danny was right behind me. He spit out his regulator and said: "Are you out of your mind Cinnamon? We could have been the next victims. All anyone on the surface had to do was follow our bubbles. So we make it easier for them by staying in one place."

"Sorry, Danny. I didn't think about that till afterward. We need to talk to the police right away."

"Let's put our stuff in the van and get out of here," Danny said. "The sooner the better."

The police station was nearby; we'd seen it while grocery shopping. While many of Zeestad's buildings featured Colonial Dutch architecture and bright colors, the police station was a drab, boxy, two-story structure. Danny and I were there in minutes.

Inside, a light-skinned black man in navy blue trousers and a white, short-sleeved shirt bearing a Bonamer PD logo sat at a desk behind the counter, working on a computer.

"There's a dead body at the Town Pier," I blurted out.

The officer looked us over carefully, his expression inscrutable. We still wore our wetsuits and booties and were dripping wet. I pushed a sodden strand of reddish-brown hair out of my eyes.

Without a word, the man rose and ambled through the door behind him. I heard him speak to someone in low tones, though I couldn't hear what he said.

Annoyed, I waited impatiently. I'd already discovered that things moved at a snail's pace on Bonamer but this was ridiculous. There was a dead body that needed recovery.

Drip, drip, drip. My booties were coated with dust. A small puddle with a sandy bottom formed on the once immaculate floor. There was a slightly larger one under Danny's feet.

The cop returned with a stack of large white towels. He dropped a couple on the puddles we'd created and handed one to each of us. He opened a gate and ushered us behind the counter. After he spread towels on the seats of two wooden chairs next to his desk, he motioned us to sit.

I collapsed on one chair, dried my face and hair, and draped the towel around my shoulders. I was shivering so much my teeth were chattering.

"I'm Officer Westwood," the man said. "Please tell me exactly what happened. Start with your name."

"I don't think you understand. There's a dead man in the water near the pier," I stammered.

"You're quite sure the man is dead?"

"Positive," I said.

"No doubt whatsoever," Danny added.

"No chance he can be revived?"

"No," Danny and I said simultaneously.

There's no hurry then is there? Please tell me your name, home address and where on the island you are staying." The officer's fingers were poised over the keyboard.

The man was absolutely maddening. Still, I didn't seem to have any choice. I answered his questions. "Cinnamon Greene. I live at 400 West 3rd Street, in Cliffview, California. Danny and I are staying at the SeaSide Inn."

Westwood looked at Danny. "Your last name and home address?"

"Decker. I live at 1342 South Orange Grove in Cliffview."

"Now tell me what happened. Every detail you can remember."

So we did. As our account tumbled out, the officer's fingers tapped the keys. He asked for clarification a couple of times. When we finished, Westwood saved the document, closed the laptop and said, "I'd like you to return to the pier with me. Did you drive here? If so, wait till I pull out of the back lot and follow me in your car."

We soon saw why he needed to go first. When we got near the

pier we found Bonamer police cars blocking the streets leading to it. One moved long enough to let Officer Westwood and Danny drive through. While we were parking, I saw two officers standing near the steps leading to the water. Westwood went up a notch in my estimation. He must have dispatched the officers when he went to get towels for us.

Westwood climbed out of his cruiser remarkably fast for someone so large and summoned the other cops to join him. After a brief conference, he motioned us nearer. "Can you take me to the body?" When we nodded he said, "Give me a few minutes to gear up."

While Westwood pulled scuba gear out of his patrol car trunk and started getting ready for the dive, Danny and I sorted through the jumble of gear in the van for our masks, fins and snorkels. We hadn't neatly packed stuff in our bags the way we usually do, we'd just tossed it inside. Compounding the problem, the van's interior light wasn't very bright. Eventually, however, we had everything we needed. Danny even managed to find his compass. We didn't take our tanks because they were nearly empty.

Westwood, Danny and I swam out from shore on the surface. When we reached the spot where Danny was sure it would be, however, the blond, blue-eyed corpse was gone.

The three of us conferred as we floated on the surface.

"It was here," Danny said. "You can see scuff marks in the sand. Did your officers see a boat or any bubbles from divers while we were gone?"

"No." Westwood put his regulator in his mouth and descended. When he returned to the surface, he explained what he wanted us to do. For 40 minutes, we ran search patterns over a large expanse of sand, with Danny and me on the surface and Westwood on the bottom. We found nothing and returned to shore.

Westwood wasn't happy. "Where did the body go?" he demanded. "Are you sure the man was dead?"

"The man was definitely dead," Danny said.

"Absolutely no question he was dead," I added.

"If I find out the two of you are playing some sort of game with us, you will leave the island immediately, never to return," Westwood threatened.

He sloshed over to his car, stripped off his gear and threw it in the trunk. He cast a malicious glance in our direction before driving out of the lot with the other two patrol cars close behind.

Danny and I were exhausted and totally confused. We bristled over Westwood's allegation.

"Can you believe it? He thinks we're making up stuff. Why would we do that?"

"We saw a body," Danny replied, "and then it was gone. Where the hell did it go?"

I had no answer for that and the short drive to the SeaSide Inn was made in silence.

Chapter 3

At the Inn we found the third member of our group, Weasel, comfortably ensconced in an easy chair, engaged in his favorite activity: lifting dip-covered chips to his mouth and drinking a soda while watching a Dodgers/Mets baseball game. True to his name, he had weaseled out of coming with us, claiming fatigue. In my opinion he wasn't quite ready to make his first night dive. He hadn't been a diver all that long.

Danny and I took turns telling him what had happened. When we finished Weasel said: "A dead body? Someone dropped a dead body on you!" That's freaky. I hope you don't expect me to dive the Town Pier any time soon."

"The pier is known for its marine creatures," I pointed out, "not dead bodies. This is probably the first and last one anyone will ever find there."

"Can I see the video?" Weasel asked.

"Shit." Danny looked at me. "We never told Westwood about the photo and video. They prove we aren't liars."

I groaned. "Last thing I want is to see Westwood again tonight. Besides, I should make copies so there are backups in case the police lose or damage the originals. I'm too tired to do that now. I'll do it first thing tomorrow."

"Can I see the video?" Weasel pleaded. Danny plugged his camera into my laptop and fast-forwarded to the part where the dead man showed up.

"Whoa!" Weasel said when it finished. "That was scary."

"Surprise, surprise," I said.

Weasel went off to bed a few minutes later. Danny and I did, too. He fell sleep instantly. Though I was exhausted, I remained wide-awake, my mind spinning.

Sometimes stretching will relax me so the sandman can do his job. Since I didn't want to disturb Danny, I went out on the balcony to do my routine. The ocean was calm, the night still. The surf lapped gently at the shore.

Stretching, however, did not have its usual effect. I just could not stop thinking about what had happened.

I had no doubt that whoever was on the boat had seen our exhaled air bubbles. The body had been dropped on us on purpose. But were the people on the boat expecting someone else to be there or did they know the bubble blowers beneath them were Danny and me?

It was weird that the body was gone when we went back with Westwood. The more I thought about it, the more certain I was that it hadn't been moved very far and we would have found it if we had expanded our search. We would have to make another one in the light of day.

Since I couldn't sleep anyway, I made copies of the one image I'd taken with my camera and the brief video I'd shot with Danny's. I uploaded them to a website Dad and I use for his business, Greene's One Stop Camera and Photo Shop. I also made copies for the police.

When I finished, I slipped into bed next to Danny and drifted off into a restless sleep.

Chapter 4

The SeaSide Inn's compressor sputtered to life at 7:00 am, rousing me from a troubled sleep. It awakened Danny, too. We lay in bed, listening to the clang of tanks being filled and loaded into boats.

My early morning hours had been punctuated by nightmares I could not recall. In the light of day, what had happened the night before made even less sense.

Danny is usually wide-awake and cheerful as soon as his eyes open. Not today. He looked as tired as I felt and he didn't whistle as he went about his usual routine. He didn't call me Sunshine, either, a name he chose because it's the opposite of what I am when I stumble out of bed.

I eventually forced myself upright and went into the kitchen. Weasel was there and, miracle of miracles, he'd made coffee. I didn't know he possessed such a skill.

Our apartment had two balconies: a large one off the living room with an ocean view and a little one off the kitchen overlooking the pool. Weasel was on the small balcony, accessed via French doors. As I sat down next to him Danny joined us, tugging a pale blue T-shirt bearing his Cliffview dive shop logo over dark blue swim trunks.

As I sipped coffee I remembered the day I met Danny on a California dive boat. Then, as now, he was the most attractive man I'd ever seen: dark blue eyes, short, curly light brown hair and a swimmer's body; lean yet nicely muscled.

My divorce wasn't final then and I had no intention of getting involved with anyone. One look at Danny, however, and I was smitten. Not that I let him know that right away.

Danny owned the only scuba diving shop in Cliffview and was a member of the Wednesday Warriors, a close knit informal group my dad and several of his friends founded a couple of decades ago. As the name indicated, they dived together once a month on a Wednesday. Danny filled their tanks, serviced their regulators, certified family members and friends, and sold them new gear when they needed it. He already knew a lot about me before we met yet he asked me out anyway. I'm not sure whether that makes him brave or foolhardy.

Danny drained his cup and went into the kitchen, returning with the carafe. "I think we should go back to the pier," he said as he poured coffee into our cups. "I don't think we searched enough area last night. The body was moved underwater. I wouldn't be surprised if..."

"...someone was watching us," I finished. Then I shuddered. "That kept me awake last night."

"We need to get to the pier," Danny said.

"I didn't sleep well," Weasel said, "I think I'll stay here and rest up."

"Oh no you don't, Weasel, we need your help," I said. "Three sets of eyes are better than two."

"Before we go, we should show the video to Ryan," Danny said. "Maybe he can identify the dead guy."

Ryan and Sara Miller bought the SeaSide Inn three years ago. It was a small resort with a U-shaped two-story building containing 20 rental units that surrounded a free form pool on three sides. We had an upstairs unit on the beach, accessed via a staircase outside the kitchen door that led to the pool deck. Across from it were a small, well-stocked dive shop and a compressor/storage room.

When I think of Ryan I see the color brown. He was in his middle 40s and had short, dark brown hair, dark brown eyes and a muscular, deeply tanned body, which looked good in his work clothes — a pair of brown or navy blue swim trunks and a SeaSide Inn T-shirt. He was about four or five inches shorter than Danny, who stands six foot one.

I met the Millers for the first time when we arrived on Bonamer. Danny had always used such superlatives when he talked about his scuba instructor that I had expected Superman. Although Ryan was most assuredly competent and intelligent, in my opinion he wasn't nearly as good looking or personable as Danny and he occasionally displayed a macho attitude I found unattractive.

Ryan had, however, accurately described the charms of Bonamer and his resort in his e-mails to Danny. They were everything he'd claimed and more. He'd invited Danny to visit — for free — when guests cancelled at the last minute and he had an empty unit. Danny invited me to come with him. When Weasel heard about the trip, he invited himself.

The three of us found Sara in front of the dive shop, sweeping tree blossoms from the sidewalk. Ryan had been her scuba instructor and their relationship deepened when the classes ended. A former kindergarten teacher eight years younger than her husband, Sara had short, curly auburn hair and unusual reddish brown/golden eyes. The Bonamer sun had turned her tall, slender body to bronze. She wore a green bikini top, a pair of matching green shorts and sandals.

"How was your night dive?" she asked.

"We were having a great time until we found a dead man," Danny answered. "We have video of him. We hope you or Ryan will be able to identify him."

Sara blanched. "A body? Oh no, I definitely do not want to see that. And Ryan's not here, he's running the morning boat."

"The video isn't gory. There's no blood or anything," I said.

Sara was not convinced.

"You don't have to watch the whole thing," I said. "Danny can freeze a frame for you. You don't have to look at anything else."

Sara hesitated but finally agreed. We went into the dive shop and Danny placed my laptop on a counter. When he found a good shot of the body, he froze it on the computer screen and called Sara over. When she looked at the photo she gasped and tightened her grip on my arm until it hurt.

"OmiGod!"

"Do you recognize him?" I asked.

"It's Neils Van Slyke, the golf course developer." Sara looked ill.

Ryan had told us about the group he helped form called No Tees that was dedicated to stopping Van Slyke from building a golf course on Bonamer.

"We told the police about the body but when we tried to take Westwood to it, it was gone," Danny explained.

"We forgot to give Westwood the video," I said. "We're taking him a copy today."

"We're going back to the pier in a few minutes," Danny added.

"We think the body is still there."

"Please," Sara said. "Don't show this to *anyone* until Ryan has a chance to see it. And please, please, don't tell anyone about it before he says it's okay."

Sara was usually pretty laidback and I was struck by her intensity.

Danny's eyebrows shot up and he glanced at me. "Okay," he said.

Back in our apartment, Weasel said, "Was Sara's reaction to the video over the top or what?'

"Way over the top," I said.

Danny didn't comment but I could see Sara's request troubled him.

We loaded our gear in the van and headed for the Town Pier. We were relieved to find we were the only divers there.

It was already hot. Eager to get out of the sun, we geared up quickly. In the water, the light of day did little to dispel my anxiety. I didn't really want to see that body again, let alone run into whoever had dropped it on us, then spirited it away.

Weasel seemed apprehensive as well, never venturing more than an arm's length away from Danny.

We located the spot where we thought the body had been, although the marks we'd seen on the sandy bottom last night were gone. The water was clear, with visibility of about 100 feet, and there was no corpse to be seen in any direction.

We headed for the pier. Before the dive, we'd decided to start at the north end and work our way to the section that connected it to shore. Danny teaches search and rescue classes. He told us what he wanted us to do and we followed his directions.

Ten minutes later we found Neils Van Slyke among the pier pilings. Now he sat cross-legged on the bottom, his ankles and wrists tied to old tires half buried in the sand. The buoyancy vest was gone and there was a white baseball cap perched jauntily on his head. The hat bore the No Tees logo; the red symbol that means "no," a blue golf tee and the words, "No Tees," also in blue.

I could barely force myself to look at the body and the marine creatures that now crept about on it. The feasting had already begun.

Keeping our distance so we didn't compromise the integrity of the crime scene, Danny and I moved around the body photographing it, I with my still camera and him with his video. Weasel watched from a few feet away.

We'd agreed that if we located the body, Danny and Weasel would stay with it while I summoned the police. When I'd taken all the photos I thought necessary, I handed my camera to Weasel and headed in, glad to be leaving.

Surprise. When I surfaced a few feet from shore, Officer Westwood and another man were walking down the concrete steps to the water, dressed in dive gear.

Westwood pulled his mask off and scowled. "What are you doing here?"

"We found the body. Danny and Weasel are making sure it doesn't disappear again. I was on my way to get you."

Westwood snorted and said something to his partner in Papiamento, Bonamer's native language. A blend of several dialects, it is incomprehensible to most visitors, including me.

Westwood glared at me. "Take us there. Then you and your friends get out of our way and let us do our jobs. No more meddling in police business. Do I make myself clear?"

I opened my mouth to protest but the angry look on Westwood's face changed my mind. "Follow me," I said and turned back to the sea.

Navigation is not my strong suit on land or underwater, which is why I usually leave it to Danny. His attempts to teach me to use a compass have been fruitless and frustrating, I am totally directionally challenged. Without GPS in my car I would cluelessly wander California freeways, never getting where I wanted to be. Now I worried about navigating the broad stretch of sand between shore and pier. Would I be able to find my buddies and the body? I breathed a sigh of relief when they came into view.

Westwood gestured to get our attention, then jabbed his finger at us and pointed toward shore. His meaning was unmistakable.

We didn't hang around to see if he'd change his mind. As we removed our fins in the shallows, Danny said, "Boy was I glad to see you. Babysitting dead bodies makes me nervous."

"I'll second that," Weasel said. "Things were nibbling on that guy."

"The officers were already on the steps when I surfaced," I explained. "Westwood was not happy to see me."

"Tough," Danny said. "He should have been in the water at daybreak."

"We've been ordered to stop meddling in police business."

"Fine with me," Danny said. "I don't need to find any more dead guys."

Weasel nodded.

A sudden thought struck me. "I wonder what happened to the anchor."

"What anchor?" Danny asked.

"The concrete cylinder with a hook on the top that was attached to the body the first time we found it. It kept Van Slyke on the bottom. I've seen one of those somewhere, I just can't think where."

Danny's face cleared. "Now I remember. It looked pretty heavy and couldn't have been easy to move. Do you want to go back and look for it?"

"And get another lecture from Westwood? Oh no. He ordered us to stay out of police business. So out we'll stay."

We removed our gear and wetsuits, wrapped towels around our bodies and loaded up the van. We arrived at the SeaSide just after the boats returned from the morning dive. Ryan, Sara and their instructor, Laurie, were busy unloading tanks and dealing with guests, so we went to our apartment to wait until they were free.

We showered and changed into dry clothes, then downloaded our photos and video and got our camera systems ready for the next dive. Lunch was iced tea, Gouda cheese, fruit and French bread, eaten on the big balcony off the living room, which provided a beautiful panoramic view of the turquoise Caribbean. It was a very pleasant day. A gentle breeze blew. The sky was blue, with a few cotton puff clouds moving slowly across it.

There was a knock on the door. "It's open," Danny yelled.

"Did you find Van Slyke?" Ryan looked really, really tense.

"Oh yeah," Danny said. "Come into the kitchen and I'll show you the videos."

We gathered around my laptop on the kitchen table and Danny began playing last night's video.

Ryan stood next to me. When the body showed up on the screen, he went rigid.

"He was dead when he was dumped on us," I said. "I didn't see any marks on the visible parts of his body and have no idea what killed him."

"Cinnamon is a part-time forensic photographer with our local police department," Danny explained.

"You're a cop?" Ryan asked.

"No. I'm a civilian employee. It's a small force with no need for a full time forensic photographer."

When the first video ended, Danny played the one he'd taken on our morning dive. I'd told him what I wanted him to do and he'd followed my directions perfectly, taking a wide angle shot of the corpse, then moving in to get close-ups of it and the yellow lines that tied the hands to the tires. When the body's head, complete with the white hat and its special logo, appeared on the screen, Ryan groaned.

"Oh shit. That's a No Tees hat. Looks like someone is trying to pin Van Slyke's death on No Tees or worse, me.

"I've got to call a meeting," he went on. "See if anybody has any ideas on damage control."

"Need help?" Danny asked.

"Yes. I'll need you to explain what you saw. I'll let you know when we decide on a place and time."

Ryan headed to the door. Just before he left the room, he turned to us. "Uh, Danny, Cinnamon. I'd appreciate it if you didn't mention these videos to anyone just yet. Okay?"

"Okay." Danny and I answered simultaneously.

A second later, Ryan was gone. In 30 minutes, the SeaSide Inn's two boats would depart for the afternoon dive. If we wanted to be on them, we'd better get ready.

On our first day we'd made our morning dive with Ryan and our afternoon dive with Laurie Cook, the only other member of his dive staff besides Sara. I preferred Laurie, who had worked for the inn's previous owner. Fluent in German, English and Papiamento, she was in her late 20s, with dark eyes and dark hair, usually worn in a long, thick braid.

Laurie was at least five feet nine inches tall with long, tan legs and a generous bust. Danny, Weasel and I enjoyed diving with her. She had an encyclopedic knowledge of Bonamer's sea creatures and conducted her dives at a leisurely pace, allowing us plenty of time to observe and photograph the creatures she found. On the boat after each dive, she would answer questions about what we'd seen and provide interesting details about the animals' lives and habits.

We were lucky on the afternoon dive. No one requested a guided dive and we had Laurie all to ourselves. Weasel got the first look at Laurie's finds. When he moved on, Danny and I would take pictures/video to our heart's content. When we finished, Laurie and

Weasel would be nearby, ready to show us something else.

The dive was a lot of fun. Danny and I were especially excited about the two seahorses, one red and one orange, that Laurie pointed out. She said if we made the morning dive with her the next day we would probably see a yellow frogfish. That was exciting. We signed up for Laurie's boat as soon as we got back to the inn.

We showered and had a snack. Weasel settled down with a mystery I'd loaned him. That was another surprise; until this trip, I'd never seen him read anything but graphic novels.

Danny and I did photo gear maintenance and made back-ups of the images we'd shot that day. We worked at the large round table in the kitchen, which was covered with our equipment: battery chargers whose cords snaked down to electrical outlets, devices to download and store digital images; strobes and back-up strobes, cameras, and last but not least, my laptop computer, which I shared with Danny.

Late that afternoon we went to the No Tees meeting. Ryan had told Danny about the organization in e-mails before we arrived on the island. He and other dive operators had founded it to oppose the construction of a golf course because they knew that growing grass on a desert island like Bonamer would involve importing soil and the liberal use of fertilizer and freshwater. The runoff would pollute the ocean, promote algae growth and kill marine life.

A golf course, Ryan had written, would mean an end to Bonamer's clean, clear waters and make a mockery of the island's license plate slogan, "Diving Paradise."

However, not everyone on the island was against building a golf course. Many thought it would increase tourism and add jobs. Van Slyke had sweetened the deal by pledging funds for an electricity-generating wind turbine park if the golf course was approved. Electricity was costly on Bonamer and the prospect of lower bills was a huge incentive to support the project.

The No Tees meeting would be held at the Green Iguana Resort, one-half mile south of the SeaSide Inn. Danny, Weasel and I walked there with Sara and Ryan along a paved, two-lane road that was nearly traffic-free.

The Green Iguana was the largest and most luxurious resort on Bonamer. It sat on a canal overlooking a small marina, both of which had been carved from coral limestone. The resort had spacious, carefully landscaped grounds and there was even a tiny casino, one of two on the island.

The outdoor bar where the No Tees meeting would be held was next to a large pool, just steps from a beautiful sandy beach (Ryan said the sand was imported from the mainland) and the ocean.

The sun had begun its slow descent in the sky by the time we arrived. We weren't the first to show up, though the only person I recognized was Laurie, who was at the bar talking to a hunky blond guy about her age.

Ryan was surrounded immediately and peppered with questions. He waved everyone off saying, "Be patient. I'll tell you everything I know at the meeting."

We found a table near the pool and ordered hors d'oeuvres and beer. Two No Tees officers joined us.

Ryan introduced the treasurer as Karin Van Slyke. She was a tall, tan woman with sun-bleached hair and a slight Dutch accent. Ryan said she ran an upscale boutique at the Green Iguana. Karin looked cool and elegant in a black tank top and white shorts, which accented her trim, athletic figure. In her late 40s, she had been beautiful. While still attractive, her fair skin showed the effects of too much sun. She seemed preoccupied and Ryan had to introduce us twice. Karin's last name was the same as the dead man's and I wondered if and how they were related.

We'd met No Tees' secretary, Lester Gudrow, when he'd dropped by the SeaSide Inn the day before. An American with a pronounced Mid-West accent, Les was a wiry dark haired man in his early 50s who worked for North Shore Diving.

The three No Tees officers retired to a corner of the room to discuss the night's agenda. People straggled in. Ryan had told us No Tees' membership included a cross section of the island's residents. By 7:00, at least 100 people were in attendance and the noise level had risen considerably.

Karin and Les returned to our table while Ryan hoisted himself up on top of the wooden bar. Seated there, he put two fingers in his mouth and whistled the meeting to order. The crowd quieted immediately.

"I know you've all heard plenty of rumors about what happened at the Town Pier," Ryan said. "It seems my friends, Danny and Cinnamon, were in the wrong place at the wrong time last night. A dead man was dropped on them from a boat, which sped off. The body was gone when they returned to the site with Officer Westwood.

"Danny and Cinnamon went back to the pier this morning and rediscovered the body. It had been moved under the pilings and a No Tees hat had been put on its head. The dead man, as you know, was Neils Van Slyke."

There was a loud murmur from the crowd. Karin started to rise, her face a ghastly white. Les put a hand on her arm and she sank back into her chair.

Ryan spoke again. "Whoever killed Van Slyke is trying to implicate No Tees. We need to decide what to do about that."

Most of the discussion that followed was not, in my opinion, very constructive. Many who spoke said they were glad Van Slyke was dead because it meant the golf course project was also dead. Les Gudrow hammered this point home several times.

The group eventually settled down after everyone had vented their feelings. They agreed a letter should be sent to the police, with a copy to the local newspaper. The letter would deny No Tees' involvement in Van Slyke's death and for emphasis, all the organization's members would sign it.

Ryan, Karin and Les took Les' laptop to an empty table to compose the letter. The others huddled in small groups to talk. Weasel wandered off to get another beer and was soon engaged in conversation with a cute young woman. Danny and I walked down to the beach.

"Is Van Slyke a common Dutch name?" I asked.

Danny shrugged. "I have no idea. Maybe Karin is Neils' sister. We'll have to ask Ryan."

He changed the subject. "Isn't this is an incredible property? Man, would I like to own something like this someday."

"Dream on," I said.

"Everybody needs dreams," Danny said. "I've got several. You can make one of them come true." Standing behind me, he put his arms around my waist and nuzzled my neck. That still makes me shiver.

We returned to the bar as the first draft of the letter was being read. Three drafts later, the majority of those present approved it. Les headed to the resort's office to print it. When he came back, people lined up to sign it. Most left afterward.

The five of us walked back to the SeaSide Inn in the dark on the dusty, uneven shoulder of the road. Every once in awhile Ryan would announce, "road apples," allowing us to avoid stepping on the dark brown nuggets left by the wild donkeys that roamed the island.

Danny asked, "Any idea who might have killed Van Slyke?"

"No," Ryan said. "He had a lot of enemies, including Karin. Did you know she was his first wife? He dumped her for a younger woman after 20 years of marriage. He was worth millions but Karin had signed a prenuptial agreement and ended up with very little.

"They traveled a lot when they were together," Ryan continued. "Karin wanted children, he didn't. She regrets giving into him on that now. She was very upset when he remarried and had two kids right away.

"I was surprised she didn't speak tonight. She's not usually shy about pointing out Neils' shortcomings."

"Les was certainly hostile," Danny said.

"Yeah, well, he's had a lot of trouble with Van Slyke," Ryan said. "Several years ago, when the island was hit by storm surge, Les' operation lost its pier, dive shop and both dive boats. He borrowed money to rebuild from Van Slyke, using his property as collateral. They agreed on monthly payments."

"Let me guess," I said. "Van Slyke raised them."

"He didn't have to," Ryan said. "They were already so high Les couldn't make them. Van Slyke waited until Les rebuilt before foreclosing and then selling the property. The new owners demanded rent beyond what Les could afford and he was forced to sell North Shore Diving to them. Now he's employed by the business he used to own and has to work for a know-nothing boss half his age."

Ryan continued. "Van Slyke was a greedy, ruthless man. Few profited from dealings with him, business or personal."

Back at the SeaSide Inn, Weasel retired to his bedroom while Danny and I took a couple of beers out on the big balcony, settled on a comfortable sofa and watched the moon rise ever higher above the calm Caribbean. I snuggled up to Danny and he put his arm around me. The sound of the surf lapping the beach was soothing — so soothing we fell asleep.

Chapter 5

Sara was awake long after Ryan drifted off to sleep because the day's events — particularly the No Tees meeting — kept roiling around in her mind. She finally slipped out of bed and went to the living room, where she sat on the couch in the dark and tried to figure out what to do about the mess she'd made of her life.

Paul was her biggest worry. She'd been surprised when he showed interest in her. Not only was she several years older, she was the wife of a man who had fired him.

From the beginning Sara had wondered if Paul flirted with her to punish Ryan. That was one of the reasons she had ignored his initial overtures.

Then someone — she couldn't think who — started sending her e-mails that claimed Ryan and Laurie were still seeing each other. The crude, graphic language brought unsettling images to Sara's mind. She'd believed Ryan when he'd said he'd only slept with Laurie once, when he'd had too much to drink one night while Sara was in California visiting her family. He claimed that when she kept extending her visit he was afraid she wasn't coming back. He swore that he loved Sara, that Laurie meant nothing to him and he would never, ever sleep with her again. Sara believed him.

Laurie, however, continued to work for the SeaSide Inn and Sara had to see her nearly every day. That was difficult. She asked Ryan to fire Laurie several times. He refused. Sara didn't tell him about the e-mails, but when first one arrived, she asked again, almost begging this time. Ryan just looked tired.

"That would be a huge mistake," he'd said. "A lot of our customers return year after year because they love diving with Laurie. You, of all people, should know how much we need the business she brings in."

Sara sighed. She couldn't stop thinking about the e-mails. And, the next time she saw Paul, she flirted back. Encouraged, he suggested they have lunch together on her day off. Sara hadn't expected that. She said no.

More e-mails alleging a Ryan/Laurie connection arrived. Sara was in a tizzy. Part of her was sure there was no affair, but a trifle of doubt remained. When Ryan and Laurie were together, she watched them like a hawk. She saw nothing extraordinary.

Since Paul had worked at the SeaSide Inn, he knew its schedule. He began calling Sara when she was alone in the dive store. Nothing she said deterred him, he insisted they get together. Finally, she gave in. If Ryan could have a fling, why couldn't she?

She didn't sleep the night before their first meeting and was too nervous to eat breakfast the next morning. She thought Ryan would notice but he didn't. She made up a story about where she was going that day, answering questions he hadn't asked.

Paul and Sara met on the other side of the island, at a restaurant she never been to before. Although she thought she wanted Ryan to find out, she was horribly anxious while they were there, fearful someone she knew would wander in and see them together. Afterward, she hurried to her car and jumped in so Paul couldn't try to kiss her.

That first meeting was so unnerving Sara nearly gave up her plan to sleep with Paul. He suggested she'd be more comfortable if they met in a private place, his condo for instance. Sara didn't like that. The condo's entrance was on a main street and there was no place to park her car where it wouldn't be seen.

Sara was conflicted. While she wanted Ryan to find out, she didn't want to broadcast what she was doing to everyone on Bonamer.

After another e-mail about Laurie and Ryan arrived, Sara screwed up her courage and asked a friend if they could use her apartment, which had an enclosed garage. The friend, who had a secret of her own, could hardly refuse.

Thus began an affair that had been difficult to initiate and became impossible to end. During one of their trysts, Sara, knowing Paul and Laurie were drinking buddies, asked (casually, she hoped), "Is Laurie having an affair with Ryan?"

"If she was, she wouldn't tell me. She's not the kiss and tell type," Paul had said. "You've got eyes, what do you think?"

That did not relieve Sara's distress.

Although they had sex, Sara and Paul were not lovers. There wasn't a shred of chemistry between them. It was a mechanical act, lacking even minuscule amounts of romance and tenderness.

Sara wasn't happy that the "dates" with Paul dragged on, with no end in sight. She thought her husband would find out right away and she could end the charade. She imagined a scenario that never materialized: Ryan would confront her, she would produce the e-mails and tell him they had driven her into Paul's arms. Ryan would be contrite, break off his affair with Laurie and fire her. Sara and Ryan would live happily ever after.

Only Ryan proved maddeningly oblivious. Sara saw Paul on her day off for several weeks. She tried dropping verbal clues about where she was going and what she was doing. Ryan didn't pick up on them.

One day, out of the blue, Sara's head cleared and she realized she'd made a colossal mistake. It began with speculation about when Ryan and Laurie could be meeting. The answer was "next to never." Ryan was at the SeaSide Inn or out on a boat 24/7. The only time he and Sara were apart was on her day off, when she ran errands and saw Paul.

Yet even then, Ryan and Laurie weren't together. When one was in the dive shop, the other was out on a boat. Laurie went home for lunch while Ryan ate in his office, hunched over his computer.

Sara knew her husband. He was obsessive-compulsive about the SeaSide Inn's business. There was no possibility that he would rendezvous with anyone during the lunch hour, not when there were things to order, e-mails to answer and bookings to be made.

The nasty e-mails had to be fabrications. Sara couldn't believe it took her so long to figure that out. Who sent them and why? Was it Laurie, hoping to establish a wedge between Sara and Ryan? If so, she had done a good job.

Once Sara had hoped Ryan would find about Paul, now she hoped he didn't. She didn't want him seeking comfort in Laurie's arms, comfort she knew Laurie would be delighted to give.

Paul had asked to see her during that night's No Tees meeting and she had agreed, intending to end the affair. They snuck out separately and went to the friend's nearby apartment. Sara was afraid someone would miss them and was anxious to get back to the

---

meeting.

Right off the bat, Sara told Paul she wasn't going to see him again. The affair was over.

"No, it's not," Paul had said, a triumphant look on his face. "If you break up with me I'll make sure the entire island finds out about us. Is that what you want?"

They had sex then, even though Sara wasn't the least bit in the mood. Paul was jubilant and enjoyed making her do things she didn't want to.

Sara returned to the meeting first, relieved to discover no one seemed to have noticed her absence. When Paul returned he had a smirk on his face.

Now Sara sighed again. She wished there was some way out of this nightmare.

Chapter 6

Nestled next to Danny on the balcony sofa, I was awakened from a deep sleep by the tinkle of breaking glass. It was not yet dawn. The noise came from the kitchen, where French doors opened onto the small balcony that overlooked the pool.

"Danny." I shook him. "Someone's in the kitchen."

He was awake instantly. "Stay here," he said in my ear. "I'll check it out."

Right. I was a step behind Danny when he opened the screen door that led to the living room. Unfortunately, it creaked.

"Yell 'fire' when I count to three," he whispered. When he reached the magic number, he switched on the overhead light in the living room.

"Fire! Fire! Fire!" we shouted.

There was a loud crash. We got to the kitchen in time to see a shadowy figure slip through the door to the stairs leading to the pool deck. The door slammed closed.

In the light that streamed into the kitchen from the living room, we saw the large round table had been up-ended. Our photo equipment was scattered across the ceramic tile floor.

We lost time trying to get to the door without stepping on anything. When Danny finally yanked it open and turned on the outside light, Ryan was at the bottom of the stairs holding a garden hose.

"Where's the fire?"

"There's no fire," I said. "Someone broke into our unit. Did you see anyone?"

Ryan dropped the hose and started up the steps. "Cancel the fire department," he yelled. "False alarm." To us he said, "Why did you yell fire? You scared the hell out of us."

"People are much more likely to help if they think there's a fire." Danny explained. "Yell 'help, help' and they'll be afraid there's a weapon involved."

As Ryan turned on the kitchen light, Sara appeared in the doorway. Danny, Ryan and I set the table upright.

"What happened?" Sara asked.

Danny filled her in as all of us picked up camera parts. Fortunately, underwater photo gear is extraordinarily rugged. I examined each piece as I placed it back on the table; while there were some dings and scratches and a dent or two, nothing was broken or looked too damaged to use, though we wouldn't know for sure until we'd put the systems together and tested them underwater.

Danny had been taking inventory of the items on the table and when he spoke his voice was full of dismay.

"Shit, Cinnamon. Your laptop and my video camera are gone."

Besides containing a lot of sensitive information I wouldn't want a thief to have, the laptop allowed us to use the internet and process our photos and video.

While the laptop was a huge loss for both of us, I felt really bad for Danny. Not being able to take videos of our dream vacation was devastating.

"Did you see the thief?" Sara asked.

"I think it was a man," Danny said.

"It was definitely a man," I said. "Shorter than Danny and wearing dark colored shorts, a dark T-shirt and a baseball cap. Not fat but not skinny, either."

Danny looked at me as if I were crazy. "You saw all that?"

"I have been trained to notice things," I replied.

"Forensic photography?" Sara asked.

"Yes. I have to observe crime scenes before I photograph them."

Ryan said: "The guy got in by breaking a pane in the balcony door. I doubt he'll be back tonight. But I can't replace the glass till tomorrow. Why don't you spend the night at our house?"

Danny and I looked at each other. "We can't leave our stuff," I said. We've already lost too much."

"And I don't want to pack and move anything tonight," Danny finished.

"Are you sure?" Ryan asked.

"Yes," we said.

"What about Weasel?" Ryan asked.

Now I realized that our roommate hadn't made an appearance. "I'll check," Danny said.

He was back a couple of minutes later. "Weasel's sound asleep."

"All the noise didn't wake him?" Sara asked.

"His air conditioner probably covered it," Danny said.

Ryan and Sara started to leave. "Shouldn't we call the police?" I asked.

"No point," Ryan answered. "We know from experience that they won't come out at this time of night. Just report the burglary at the station in the morning."

After the Millers left, I swept up the glass from the broken window, noting that it was on the balcony, not in the kitchen. I was about to point this out to Danny when he said: "Want to help me move the sofa against the French doors?"

And so I did. Someone could still probably get in but the ear-splitting screech the couch legs made on the tile floor should awaken us.

When we finished, we sank into our bed. I didn't think I'd be able to sleep, but I did.

All the while Weasel slumbered on, oblivious to the events taking place outside his bedroom door.

Chapter 7

Neither Danny nor I heard the compressor start the next morning, though it surely did. Instead, it was an insistent pounding on our front door that awakened us.

Danny stumbled out of bed to answer it, wrapping a towel around his waist. I pulled on a bathing suit and pair of shorts and followed him.

Officer Westwood and one of his deputies stood in the kitchen. Even through sleepy eyes I could see he was angry. He held a newspaper in one hand.

"Did it ever occur to you to keep your mouth shut about what you saw?" he demanded, waving the newspaper in the air. "Now everyone on the island knows every detail about the discovery of the body. How are the police supposed to carry out an investigation?"

With a small leap, I swiped the newspaper from Westwood's hand and unfolded it. There, on the front page, was an article on the No Tees meeting. Right next to it was an accurate but lurid account of both times we found Van Slyke's body. It was not complimentary to the Bonamer Police Department. The article's source was said to be "a confidential informant who was not authorized to speak about the incident."

Danny read the article over my shoulder. "I didn't talk to anyone about any of this."

I glanced at the byline. It wasn't a name I recognized. "I never heard of this woman. I definitely did not talk to her," I said.

Westwood wasn't appeased. "The article claims you have photographs and videos of the body, something you never mentioned to the police." Westwood was livid now. "I want that material now."

"I told you I worked with my home town police department as a forensic photographer when you interviewed us at the station," I said. "In all the excitement I simply forgot to mention I had taken one photo and a short video of the body. I would have given you copies of them yesterday if you hadn't ordered me to stay out of police business."

"By the way, our apartment was burglarized last night. The thief stole my laptop and Danny's video camera and dumped all of our photo equipment on the floor. He got in by breaking one of the glass panes in the French doors."

Westwood strode over to the doors and pushed the couch aside so he could examine the broken windowpane.

"I want to see a report on this so-called burglary as soon as you can get down to the station. And I want the originals of what you shot now. If you are lying to me about any of this, you'll be spending time in the Bonamer jail," Westwood threatened.

I went into the bedroom and returned with a thumb drive containing the video and photo Westwood wanted. When I handed it to him, he turned and stalked out of the room. There was a loud bang as a gust of wind blew the door shut behind him.

"The only people who knew all the details in this article were you, me, Ryan and Sara," I said, indicating the newspaper. "And oh yes, Weasel," I added.

Danny looked at me.

"Weasel," we said simultaneously.

"Who do you suppose he was talking to in the bar last night?" I asked. "And what do you think they were they talking about?"

"Let's go ask him," Danny said.

Weasel, however, was not in his room. That's when we realized how late it was.

"The dive boats left an hour ago. He must have gone out on one of them," I said, adding, "Ryan and Sara didn't want the police to see that video. They are going to be upset that Westwood has a copy of it and the photo I shot."

"Nothing we can do about that. We had no choice," Danny said.

We ate breakfast in silence as I compiled a list with the names and phone numbers of my credit card company and bank. I'd need to notify them my computer had been stolen. I would call the companies to report the burglary when we went into town. Before the end of the day I'd need to borrow a laptop from Weasel or the SeaSide Inn so I could change the passwords on several websites.

I also put my photo system together. In the light of day, I found more dings and dents but once assembled, it worked.

A thought occurred to me. "There must be rental equipment on the island," I said. "Maybe you can rent a camera and housing."

Danny brightened. "I'll ask Sara."

His mood was a lot lighter after he talked to her.

"She recommended this place," he said, handing me a business card. "She thinks I can rent a system fairly cheap."

"Did you tell her Westwood has the video?"

"Yes. She wasn't happy."

"When is she ever?"

The center of Bonamer's main town, Zeestad, was only half a mile from the SeaSide Inn. Danny and I walked there along a dusty road under a very hot sun. Our first stop was the police station, where we reported the burglary. Westwood did not make an appearance.

Later, I used a public phone to alert my Cliffview bank and a credit card company about the laptop theft. This was one of those rare occasions when my lack of financial resources was a good thing. It meant fewer organizations to contact.

While I was doing that, Danny went to the camera store. I got there as he completed the paperwork for a camera/housing rental. While disappointed that it wasn't as sophisticated as the one that had been stolen, Danny thought it would do. Back at the inn I was happy to hear him whistle as he put the system together.

We had enjoyed our first dive off the SeaSide Inn's pier and decided to make another. The day was pure paradise: bright sun and crystal-clear, bathtub-warm water.

I jumped off the end of the pier first. I'd worked up a sweat getting ready in the hot sun and even though the water was 80°F it felt wonderfully cool.

Danny quickly joined me. The two of us sank to the bottom and headed for the drop-off, which was about 100 yards offshore. We swam side by side through water so warm, clear and calm it made you wish you could stay down forever. We stopped briefly to examine a large anchor and continued on.

A forest of feathery, pale green soft corals, four to five feet tall, grew along the top of drop-off. It was a very busy place. Little fish darted in and out among the corals. A small school of blue and yellow fish moved slowly in unison. I spied a reddish-brown trumpetfish. The long slender fish hung nearly vertical, tail up, head down trying to look like a branch of the soft corals it was hiding among.

The drop-off sloped gently to 90 feet, where a broad sandy plateau stretched as far as the eye could see. Fifteen feet away a small school of tarpon, five to six feet long, hovered over the sand. As we swam toward them, the silvery fish moved slowly out to sea, maintaining the distance between us. We returned to the drop-off and slowly worked our way up it. At 30 feet we encountered a green turtle about two feet long. When she saw us, the creature used her powerful front flippers to make a quick getaway.

Danny led us south along the drop-off, navigating among mounds of star corals. I photographed a juvenile spotted drum swimming in circles in a little niche under one coral head. The tiny black and white fish had a long, curving dorsal fin that floated in the water like a feather. When I finished, Danny moved in to shoot a few minutes of video.

I've been a photographer since childhood, learning the trade from my dad, "Red" Greene, owner of Greene's One Stop Camera and Photo Shop in Cliffview, a small town on the California coast between Ventura and Santa Barbara. Greene's is the only store of its type for miles. Besides selling photographic equipment and supplies, we offer a wide variety of related services, including studio portraits and photography or videography of any special event from a wedding to a birthday party — animal or human — to a bar mitzvah. The store includes a gallery of underwater photos we've taken and we sell those, too.

Long before my mother died, Dad was my primary caregiver and I went everywhere with him. I began assisting him on photo shoots when I was in elementary school. By the time I was a teenager, I was photographing special events on my own.

Dad is also the reason I became a diver. I got certified as a teenager after going out on boats with him for years. I began taking underwater photos not long afterward.

Danny, on the other hand, had only been a videographer for a few months. When we started diving together in California I would bring two camera systems underwater, one for stills and one for video. Danny would carry the one I wasn't using.

Once, while I was busy shooting a school of barracuda, a juvenile harbor seal appeared and began to play hide and seek with

Danny. The creature would glide in and out among the kelp fronds, peeking at Danny. When he stretched out on the rocky bottom and remained motionless, the seal came closer and closer to investigate. That's when Danny turned on the camera. He got wonderful footage of the seal sniffing the dome port and performing graceful acrobatics.

Later, on the boat, Danny could hardly wait to show his footage, which got raves from the other divers, including me. I was amazed. Who knew he had such talent? Soon my video system was spending more time in his hands than mine. Though I missed it, I was really happy that the man I loved had developed an interest in something else I loved. I gave him the system for his birthday and resigned myself to shooting stills until I could afford a new one.

Time passes very quickly underwater. We heard two boats in the distance, probably Laurie's and Ryan's, returning from their morning dives. Otherwise, it was quiet and serene with only our exhalations breaking the silence. We'd been down awhile when Danny indicated it was time to turn around. We swam back to the pier at a leisurely pace.

By now Sara would have told Ryan that Westwood had the video. I wondered how he'd taken the news.

All was quiet at the SeaSide Inn when we climbed out of the ocean. The four divers eating lunch in the gazebo wanted to know what we'd seen and we, in turn, asked them what sites their boats had visited and if anything unusual had occurred.

Next there was the gear rinsing and storing ritual and a quick shower on the pool deck. We wrapped colorful beach towels around our bodies and headed upstairs, cameras in hand.

Ryan darted out of the dive shop. "I have to talk to you."

"Come on up, we're about to have lunch. Have you eaten?" Danny asked.

"Yeah, yeah," Ryan said. "By the way, I'll replace the broken glass in the French door after the next dive."

Weasel was in the kitchen, making a pitcher of lemonade. Before we could say hello to him, Ryan spoke. "Sara said Westwood was here this morning. What was that about?"

"He was mad because there was an article in the newspaper about us finding Van Slyke's body," I said. "And he was furious we had a photo and video he hadn't seen."

I was observing Weasel out of the corner of my eye. He nearly

—

dropped the pitcher.

"I read the article," Ryan said, "Who talked to that reporter?"

Weasel paled.

"Who were you with in the bar last night?" I asked him.

"Me?" Weasel stirred the lemonade. "Just some girl."

"What was her name?" Ryan demanded.

"Jenny something."

"Short, dark hair, big boobs?"

"That sounds like her."

Ryan sighed. "She's on the newspaper staff. Did you happen to mention Van Slyke's body?"

"She was really interested in that."

"We have more bad news," Danny said. "Westwood demanded the video and photo we shot the night we found the body."

"Sara told me. But wasn't it in the camera and laptop that were stolen?"

"Stolen when?" Weasel asked. "Would someone please tell me what's going on?"

I told him about the break-in.

Weasel recoiled. "Wow. I saw the couch against the door this morning and wondered why it was there. I slept really well last night. The air conditioner was on and I didn't hear a thing. I guess I better turn it off at night so I..."

Ryan interrupted him. He looked at me. "You don't have the photo and video of the first time you found the body, do you? They were stolen, right?"

"They are on the stolen laptop," I said. "However, I'd already made copies. I gave a set to Westwood this morning."

Ryan sank into a chair by the kitchen table and put his head in his hands. "Damn."

"What's wrong?" Danny asked.

Ryan didn't answer at first. Then he said, "Do you remember what Van Slyke was tied to the first time you found him?"

"A cylinder with a hook on the top." I said.

"Yes," Ryan said. He visibly summoned his strength, though I could see it took considerable effort. "That was one of several identical concrete cylinders made by the former owner of the SeaSide Inn. He used them and an old anchor chain to make the decorative fence that separates our yard from the beach."

As soon as he said that, I saw the fence in my mind's eye.

Danny had commented on it as we sat on the Miller's patio, sipping cocktails and watching the sun set our first night on Bonamer.

"Is one of the cylinders missing?" I asked.

"Yes," Ryan replied. "I don't know how anyone could have gotten it off our beach without our knowing. The damn things weigh about 30 pounds.

"There's only one fence like that on the island," he went on. "Someone on the Bonamer police force will know where that cylinder came from when they see it on the video. They'll think I killed Van Slyke."

I opened my mouth to speak but Danny beat me to it. "Westwood asked for a copy. We didn't really have a choice, Ryan."

"It's my fault," Weasel said. "It never occurred to me that woman worked for a newspaper."

A look of pure misery settled on Ryan's face. He turned and left the room. Danny, Weasel and I took our lunch out on the living room balcony.

"What do you think?" I asked.

"Someone wants to frame Ryan and discredit No Tees," Danny said. "He's afraid they are going to succeed."

"I'm not so sure Ryan is innocent," I said, remembering something I had almost forgotten. "The glass from the broken window was outside on the balcony, which means the pane was broken from the inside. Ryan has a key to our unit. I think he took the computer and camera because he thought they contained the only copies of the video and photo. Then he broke the window, upended the table and ran."

"Ryan could have used his key when we were gone," Danny pointed out.

"He was afraid we would give the police the video before he could to do that," I said. "He's the same height as the thief. He was on the stairs when we opened the door. I asked him if he'd seen anyone and he didn't answer."

"I don't believe it," Danny said. "Ryan wouldn't steal my stuff. He's my friend."

"That may be true. But he's involved in this somehow, Danny. I just know it."

Chapter 8

Danny and I had to scramble to get ready for the afternoon boat. There was no time for a proper lunch, we would have to eat en route to the dive site. Weasel munched on fruit, cheese and crackers as he assembled a bag of food for us. He grabbed three bottles of water as we went out the door.

There was a blackboard outside the dive shop where guests signed up for dives, using the numbers on the scuba tanks they were issued when they checked into the SeaSide Inn. Before we made our morning dive, I'd signed all of us up for Ryan's 1:30 boat because Laurie's only had one spot left. To my surprise, Weasel had erased his number from Ryan's boat and added it to Laurie's. Just before they left the dock he tossed me our lunches and bottles of water.

I wasn't thrilled about having Ryan as our guide. When he and Danny get together an Alpha male syndrome kicks in, turning my boyfriend into someone I barely recognize.

There were eight passengers on our boat. When Ryan asked for destination suggestions, four people suggested a dive site on the southwest side of Little Bonamer.

The waters surrounding Bonamer and Little Bonamer form a marine park from the shoreline to depths of 200 feet. Sixty mooring buoys mark the main island's dive sites; there are an additional 24 around Little Bonamer, which is a mile off its big sister's western coast. The moorings are in 20 to 30 feet of water, often on a broad, sandy plateau.

Many resort operations require guests to dive with a guide and limit how deep they can go and how long they can stay down. The SeaSide Inn subscribed to the concept of "diving freedom," which meant guests went off on their own and determined their own depth and time limits. All Ryan, Laurie or Sara did was provide a brief orientation to the site.

Not everyone wants that freedom, however. Some guests feel more comfortable diving with a guide. I had been hoping Ryan would be occupied with a guest or two. Since that didn't happen, Ryan suggested he, Danny and I dive together.

Danny and Ryan helped everyone else off the boat, then the three of us back rolled off it and drifted to the bottom. The guys immediately headed for the drop-off at a breakneck pace. On a previous dive, I had tried to keep up. This time I didn't bother; the guys had longer, stronger, testosterone driven legs. Besides, you can't take photos if you're sprinting.

Like many experienced underwater photographers, I've done my share of solo diving. Since Danny and I had begun dating, however, he and I usually buddied up. It was fun to share underwater experiences and talk about them afterward. It was also great to dive with someone who could navigate. It was irritating now to have Danny leave me without so much as a backward glance. I tried to get over it.

I followed the drop-off to 50 feet and cruised along it, looking for photo subjects. The site had a number of large, bright orange elephant ear sponges, each uniquely shaped. Some were three to five feet in diameter.

I poked among the coral heads, finding a green moray eel in one shallow cave and a large, curious lobster in another. Game taking is illegal in the marine park. Most of the animals are not afraid of divers and do not seem to mind being photographed.

As luck would have it, when my air was low and I ascended to the shallows at the top of the drop-off, I saw several divers heading back to the boat and tagged along behind them. While I'm sure I could have found my own way back I was relieved that there was no need to do so.

Danny and Ryan were already on board when I climbed out of the water. I said nothing about having been deserted. I rationalized that Danny could dive with me any time but his dive time with Ryan was limited.

While we waited for the rest of the divers to return, Ryan made several jokes about my inability to keep up with him and Danny. Being left behind, he implied, meant I was in poor physical shape. I bit back a sharp retort. After all, we were staying at Ryan's resort for free. Danny looked uncomfortable but made no attempt to defend me. When I glared at him he looked away.

After the boat docked, we rinsed our gear and put it in our lockers. Danny went into the dive shop to talk to Ryan and I went upstairs to shower. Weasel had just finished his and was toweling his hair dry.

"How was your dive?" I asked.

"Terrific," he enthused. "I may have to take up underwater photography. Laurie showed me so many cool things. Have you ever seen a secretary fish?"

After he described his dive in detail, I told him about mine.

When Danny finally joined us he said, "We've been invited to dinner at the Miller's. You too, Weasel."

"Count me out," Weasel said. "Laurie and I are going diving. She wants to show me the chain moray that lives under the SeaSide's pier."

Danny and I stared at him.

"You're making a night dive? A beach night dive?" I asked.

"Off the pier," Weasel pointed out. "No surf, no sand."

"You've never made three dives in one day," Danny said.

Weasel was smug. "There's a first time for everything."

While I downloaded images and set batteries to charge, I reflected on my friendship with Weasel.

We'd lost touch when I decided to divorce his best friend, Ted, a celebrity photographer whose business I had set up and was managing in Hollywood. The last straw was seeing Ted and his girlfriend canoodle on a late night TV show they had no idea I would watch.

I moved back to Cliffview and went to work for my dad. More than a year passed, during which I didn't see or hear from Weasel. And then one day he showed up at Greene's One Stop Camera and Photo Shop. He explained he'd re-enrolled at Santa Barbara's Windgate Institute of Photography, which was where I'd met him and Ted. He intended to finish work on his degree at long last and had rented a small apartment in Cliffview.

Dad had always liked Weasel. He offered him a part-time job as a sales associate on the spot.

"What were you thinking?" I asked him later. "This is Weasel, Dad. Major flake."

"You underestimate him, honey. We deal with a lot of local

people we know well. They don't want an aggressive salesperson trying to sell them something every time they come in here. Sometimes they just want to browse or catch up on the latest gossip. Weasel is low key, patient and good with people. He's smart. Once he gets familiar with our stock he'll do fine."

Dad was right. Weasel showed up for work on time and paid close attention when I showed him what we sold and the services we offered. He did surprisingly well (at least I was surprised) on the sales floor.

Weasel slipped into my personal life as well. Danny liked him and was pleased when Weasel signed up for one of his scuba certification classes. That was another surprise. Who knew Weasel could swim? Soon the three us were diving together on the weekends and having dinner together once or twice week, usually at Danny's house. We all pitched in to buy food, cook and clean up.

Weasel's spring break coincided with our trip to Bonamer and neither of us minded when he invited himself to come along. Since he wasn't into underwater photography, Weasel traveled light. Danny and I were delighted to take advantage of that. Weasel's luggage carried some of our stuff and saved us overweight charges.

Chapter 9

The Miller's one story house was surrounded by a large dirt yard with a couple of shade trees. Ryan answered my knock and led us through the house to the patio on the beach. I took special note of the concrete cylinder/anchor chain fence that ran along the narrow stretch of rocky shore. A cylinder from one end of the fence was missing and the chain rested on the ground. I had no doubt it was the one Neils had been tied to the first time I saw him underwater.

The yard was surrounded on three sides by a six-foot high, whitewashed stone and concrete wall. A large inflatable boat was propped against one section of it.

Coals glowed in the used brick barbecue. Ryan invited us to sit in the wicker chairs arranged around a glass-topped table and took our drink orders. A gloomy Sara requested a glass of white wine, Danny and I asked for Dutch beer.

After a few minutes of small talk, Sara said she needed to work on dinner. I followed her into the kitchen, which was cooled by an overhead fan.

At my request, Sara put me to work. There was a large dining room off the kitchen. As I placed mats, plates and silverware on the table I said, "You are so lucky to live here. It is truly paradise. I envy you."

Sara frowned and emptied a package of frozen green beans into a pot of boiling water. "It's not all fun and diving, there are disadvantages. I know the crime here doesn't compare to that in big U.S. cities but still, thieves steal everything that's not nailed down to feed their drug habits. And the police don't seem able to do anything about it.

"This is a desert island in the middle of the ocean. Everything, and I do mean everything, is imported," she continued, scrubbing four potatoes with a vegetable brush. "I'm a vegetarian. Bonamer's produce comes by ship and it's at least a week old when it gets here. The selection is limited. I really, really miss all those things I took for granted in California: avocados, tomatoes, peaches, strawberries, lettuces other than iceberg and carrots that don't come in a plastic bag."

She jabbed holes in the potatoes with a fork and placed them in the microwave, then punched a couple of buttons. The oven cycled on.

"There are inexplicable shortages, too," Sara continued. "I love cheese. Sometimes all that's available is cheese in a jar, cream cheese or individually-wrapped rubber cheese slices."

Sara warmed to her subject. "We have two cats yet there wasn't a bag of kitty litter anywhere on the island for two months last year. That's so frustrating. The possible shortages make you hoard things. You should see how much toilet paper we have.

"Don't even get me started on the lack of services. If something breaks, you fix it or get a friend to fix it. There is no automobile association to call if your car won't start or has a flat tire. Parts for anything mechanical or electrical have to be ordered and can take months to arrive. When one of our outboard motors needed a part, Ryan had to fly to Miami to get it."

Sara was really wound up. I tried to derail her. "Is your family in California?" Unfortunately, that turned out to be a sore spot, too.

"Yes," Sara said. "My sister and I used to be really close. We're in e-mail contact every day but it's not the same as seeing her in person. I've only been home twice since we moved to Bonamer. Airfare is so expensive. Besides, we can't afford to hire any more staff and Ryan needs me here."

We hadn't heard Ryan come in and both of us jumped when he said, "No one wants to hear you whine, Sara." Turning to me he added, "Don't encourage her rants, she does just fine on her own." Then he announced, "The steaks will be ready in five minutes."

Sara colored but all she said was, "What would you like to drink with dinner, Cinnamon? Wine, water, iced tea?"

There was little conversation as we devoured canned fruit cocktail, steaks — Sara had a homemade veggie burger — baked potatoes and green beans. Over ice cream sundaes Ryan asked, "Whatever happened to that sweet little wife of yours, Danny? She was great."

I was shocked he would ask a question like that. Was he drunk? Danny's wife had divorced him when she found out he'd cheated on her. The breakup was painful and Danny truly regretted having caused it. He paused and visibly collected himself before saying, "Cindy's remarried and lives in San Francisco. She had twins a few months ago."

"You should never have let her go," Ryan went on. "She was a treasure." He turned to me. "I'm sure you've already discovered she left very big shoes to fill."

The words hurt. I knew Danny had loved Cindy and though I knew he loved me now, I couldn't help wondering every once in a while if he ever missed her.

Sara looked appalled. "Really, Ryan."

"I would never try to fill anyone's shoes," I said stiffly. What the hell was the matter with him?

I could see Ryan's comments had upset Danny, too, though he didn't say anything. Conversation died. Not long after, we said our good-byes and headed for our apartment. Weasel wasn't there and we were alone for once.

"He can't still be night diving," I said.

"Sure he can," Danny said. "But he and Laurie may not be in the water."

"Weasel and Laurie? Sleeping together?"

"Why not?"

We took glasses of ice-cold lemonade out on balcony while I considered that question. If Weasel and Laurie were diving in the ocean, it wasn't in front of the SeaSide Inn. There were no lights poking through the water anywhere.

The trade winds that caressed Bonamer had swept the clouds away. The moon and a full complement of stars shone in a black velvet sky.

"I don't know what got into Ryan," Danny said. "I think he met Cindy once, very briefly, when she came to pick me up after one of my certification classes. I have no idea why he said what he did."

"He came into the kitchen as Sara was complaining about life on Bonamer," I said. "He seemed to think I had encouraged her to discuss the pitfalls of living here, which I hadn't."

"His comments were offensive. He knows I feel obligated because we're here for free and he's taking advantage of it. Still, I should have said something," Danny admitted.

"Yes, you should have. Since we're discussing Ryan, I have a question. Why does a dive with the two of you become a race? Who cares who can swim the fastest? That isn't what diving is about."

"Ryan has always been super competitive," Danny said. "After he certified me, we made several lobster dives together. They weren't fun. He had to be first in the water at every site. By the end of the day, he had to have caught either the biggest bug or the most bugs on the boat, preferably both. If that didn't happen, it was my fault. I got tired of that pretty quickly and told him he'd have to find another buddy. Since we wouldn't be game hunting here, I thought things would be different. They're not."

"Well, I won't be diving with the two of you ever again," I said. "Don't even bother to ask."

"Don't worry," Danny said. "We swam so fast it was impossible to shoot video. I've already told Ryan his dive style is incompatible with mine."

"How did he take that?" I asked.

"He said, 'You can't cut it anymore, can you?' I said, 'You're absolutely right, Ryan.'"

Danny paused. "You and Sam are the best things in my life. You know that, don't you?"

"Usually I know it. You, however, haven't asked me to marry you recently."

"What, last week wasn't recent? Besides, you always say no."

"That doesn't mean you should stop asking. How do you know I haven't changed my mind?"

Danny sighed. "Okay. Cinnamon, will you marry me?"

"No," I said.

Danny laughed. "Rejected again. Now I'll be too depressed to sleep."

"A little physical activity might cure that." I moved closer.

"You want to go for a swim in the ocean?" Danny asked, acting innocent.

"That is not what I meant and you know it." I climbed onto his lap and kissed him.

Luckily, it was dark on the balcony and there were no neighbors to spy on us.

Chapter 10

Laurie sat in front of the mirror on her dresser, combing the tangles out of her long dark hair, which was wet from the shower she'd taken after her night dive with Weasel.

Why, she wondered, did she keep falling for guys who weren't free? Before Ryan there was that Green Iguana dive instructor. When they got together in December, he claimed he was going to leave his wife and two kids as soon as the holidays were over. In January he said they couldn't possibly split until after his wife's birthday in March. That came and went, as did several more excuses. His declarations that he wasn't sleeping with his wife proved false; she got pregnant with their third child during his and Laurie's affair. When Laurie found out, she broke up with him. Still, she'd wasted almost a year on him.

Now she was "sort of" involved with Ryan. It was "sort of" because they were never alone to act on their feelings. If Sara wasn't breathing down their necks, which was nearly always, there'd be someone or something else vying for Ryan's attention. Laurie thought he acted polite but distant around her to mask his true feelings. While that might fool everyone else she knew he cared for her.

Sara was always threatening to move back to the States. Laurie hoped she'd do that soon so she and Ryan could be together. Until then, however, she had to be satisfied with memories of the one night they'd spent together. Unfortunately, she'd gotten so drunk she didn't remember much about it, although she was pretty sure they'd made love.

Laurie thought about her night dive with Weasel. It had been fun. She liked new divers because they were so enthusiastic and more than a little bit awed by her knowledge of the ocean and its inhabitants.

Weasel was a sponge and he learned quickly. But if he hoped to be Cinnamon and Danny's diving equal some day he had a long way to go. They had a big head start.

Weasel was a nice guy — cute and sort of sweet — but also rather bland and ordinary. No Mr. Excitement there. She was pretty sure he was hung up on Cinnamon, though she doubted Cinnamon had any idea he had a crush on her. She only had eyes for Danny. Now there was someone Laurie could definitely go for. She had tried flirting with him when Cinnamon wasn't around but got nowhere. In fact, the friendliness he'd shown till then had all but disappeared. Laurie figured a lot of girls hit on him and he was tired of it.

Laurie examined her reflection in the mirror, turning this way and that. There was no question she was attractive. She had big brown eyes and a nice smile. Her figure was her greatest asset, however. Guys loved those big boobs and long legs.

While Laurie had no trouble meeting men and getting their attention, few measured up to her high standards. Over the years, she'd dated most of the single guys on Bonamer, finding all of them lacking in one department or another. She'd felt so sorry for Les after his wife deserted him that she'd gone out with him a couple of times. Both of them quickly realized the age difference between them was too great and they became good friends instead of lovers.

That's more than she could say about Paul. Laurie had had high hopes for him. He was super attractive and her age, not to mention from a wealthy family. She soon discovered that although he was okay sober, he was a mean drunk. And alcohol wasn't his only vice.

Laurie and Paul had been dating for about six weeks when she found out he was also into drugs. That was something she would not tolerate. She dumped him.

His reaction surprised her. She doubted he really cared for her and figured he was upset solely because it was she who did the rejecting. Macho Paul was supposed to be the one in charge, not her. He kept pestering her for a second chance. No way that was going to happen.

While they weren't a couple any more, Bonamer's small size made it impossible to avoid Paul, especially since they hung out with the same people at the same bar. There were times Laurie ended up drinking with Paul. She was careful not to drink so much, however, that she was tempted to go home with him.

Laurie met a lot of male tourists. No point in dating them. They might love you today but they'd be gone tomorrow and you'd probably never hear from them again. Besides, truth took a holiday while they were on vacation and they lied about their marital status and just about everything else.

Ryan was definitely a cut above the rest, well worth waiting for. Laurie got all tingly when he called her "Babe," which he did frequently. She had no idea what he saw in Sara. She was skinny and flat chested, though she had a pretty face and okay hair. It was unfortunate that Sara had found out Laurie and Ryan had slept together. That really bothered her. She wanted Ryan to fire Laurie. Well, Laurie had made sure that wasn't going to happen any time soon.

If only Sara would go back to the States. Why she stayed on Bonamer was a mystery because she complained incessantly about living there. Laurie had heard those complaints so many times she knew them by heart: Sara missed her family. There wasn't any fresh fruit or vegetables. The stores were out of cheese/kitty litter/toilet paper/her favorite tea/etc.

Get over it, Laurie thought. It's an island in the middle of the ocean, for God's sake. You can't have everything.

That brought her back to Ryan. Laurie really didn't need a lot. If she had him, her life would be complete.

Chapter 11

Further news about Van Slyke's death was nonexistent. The Bonamer police released no information whatsoever and there were apparently no journalists around to ferret out the truth. Too bad the local newspaper couldn't import just one or two of the many who lived in the LA area and were now out of work because of staff cutbacks. An hour after they set foot on the island they'd be doing stand-ups in front of the police station and we'd know exactly what was going on.

The only bit of news came from Ryan, who said he'd heard that a pathologist had flown over from Curacao and completed an autopsy. I called Westwood several times, hoping to hear the results. He was never available to talk to me.

Also, someone who knew someone told Sara that Neils' widow and children were in Holland, attending to an elderly parent who was in ill health. Though devastated by her husband's death, the widow would not be returning to Bonamer until that situation was resolved.

Meanwhile, Danny, Weasel and I settled into a busy but comfortable routine. We were awakened by the SeaSide Inn's compressor, had breakfast, finished putting camera systems together, carted gear down to one of the boats and headed out for the morning dive. Danny helped cast off the lines when the boat left the dock and tied it to the mooring buoy at the dive site. He also made sure the boat was secured to the dock when we returned to the SeaSide Inn. He'd spent summers and weekends working on dive boats in high school and college and had his captain's license.

The interval between the morning and afternoon dives allowed me just enough time to download images and grab a quick lunch.

After the second dive it was again time to rinse gear and

maintain camera systems. Danny and I usually kept electronic logs of our dives, but the loss of my laptop made that impossible. We bought paper logbooks in the SeaSide Inn's tiny dive store and reverted to old-fashioned, handwritten entries.

Although we could have gone to the internet café in town Weasel insisted we use his laptop as if it was ours. Bonamer had free wireless internet and sending e-mails from a balcony overlooking a turquoise sea and a sky dotted with fluffy white clouds was the epitome of the Caribbean experience.

Our day was often capped by a night dive. After that we'd plug batteries in to charge, shower and fall into bed, happy as the proverbial clams. Sometimes Danny and I had the energy to make love, sometimes not.

We saw little of Weasel. Although he slept at our place and ate quick breakfasts and lunches there, he went out on Laurie's boat and spent every evening with her. He did not talk about their relationship and my attempts to elicit information went nowhere.

When Danny and I were out on Laurie's boat, she and Weasel always found a way to avoid diving with us. One of them would discover a problem with his or her gear at the last minute and Laurie would say, "You go ahead, we'll join you later," which of course they never did. We'd lost our critter finder.

When Ryan or Laurie had a day off, Sara ran one of the boats. Although she didn't have a cache of creatures at every site like Laurie, she was very much at home in the water and a very competent boat captain.

On one trip back to the SeaSide Inn, I stood next to her at the helm, bending close to make myself heard over the noise of the engine. "Why don't you do this more often?" I asked. "You seem to enjoy it."

"Wish I could," Sara told me. "It's boring being in the dive shop. It isn't all that busy. Also, it's small and I'm a bit claustrophobic."

"Talk to your boss," I suggested.

"He knows how I feel." Sara didn't look at me. "He says Laurie needs to go out on the boats with the guests. After all, she's the reason many of our customers return year after year."

"You could alternate with Ryan," I pointed out.

"He keeps saying that will happen," Sara said. "So far it hasn't."

Dinner out sounded good one night and we asked Sara where to go. She suggested a new, inexpensive Mexican restaurant on the east side of town.

The much larger GrapeTree Resort on the SeaSide Inn's north side has a walkway running through it that connects to a shoreline sidewalk that leads to Zeestad, Bonamer's largest town and home to most of the island's 14,000 residents.

Bonamer is 24 miles long and three to seven miles wide. The island has direct flights to and from Amsterdam and a number of Dutch citizens own vacation or retirement homes on the island.

Hand in hand Danny and I ambled along. The sun was setting over Little Bonamer, where we'd made our afternoon dive.

Life here moves at a slow pace. Although there is high-speed internet, cable TV, cell phones and ATMs, there are no roads wider than two lanes and no stoplights.

Many of Bonamer's buildings are painted blue, mustard yellow, red, pink or green and have red roofs. I made a mental note to bring my camera with me next time I went into town and take some photos.

The Mexican restaurant proved a good choice. The food was equal to that of Juanita's, one of our favorite restaurants in Cliffview, and the service was excellent.

On our trip back to the SeaSide Inn, we walked along the main road that ran through Zeestad's shopping district. The major attraction was a shopping mall one-half block long. Two stories high and painted pink with white trim, it contained minuscule shops that sold jewelry, souvenirs, beachwear and T-shirts. There was also a unisex hair salon, the photo store where Danny had rented a camera/housing, a cellular phone store and an internet café.

At its western end, the mall opened onto a tiny food court with three fast food restaurants. On the harbor across the street from it was a small, open-air bar. A steel band was playing and the place was packed.

As we crossed the street to the sidewalk leading back to the GrapeTree, I recognized Karin Van Slyke sitting with a group of people. When she saw us, she wiggled her fingers in greeting. Laurie was at another table with three men — Weasel, Les Gudrow and the blond Adonis I'd seen her with at the No Tees meeting. Tonight he wore a tight, light blue tank top that set off his tan and matched his eyes.

"Come join us!" Laurie yelled. Weasel looked unhappy.

"You up for this?" Danny asked.

"Sure."

Les grabbed a couple of empty chairs and the six of us squeezed shoulder to shoulder around the miniature table. We were lucky the band decided to take a break just then. Conversation would have been impossible while they were playing.

"You know Les Gudrow," Laurie said. "And this is Paul. He and Les both work at North Shore Diving."

"Have you been there long?" I asked Paul.

"Only since Ryan fired me," he said. His speech was slurred.

"You deserved to be fired," Laurie said. "You were always late and didn't show up at all one day."

She stumbled over the pronunciation of "deserved" and I realized Laurie had also had too much to drink. Good thing tomorrow was her day off.

"The only reason Ryan gave me the boot instead of you," Paul said, "is because you slept with him."

"Shut up, Paul," Laurie said.

Les had been watching Laurie and Paul, a disgusted look on his face. Now he drained his beer, pushed his chair back and announced, "Time to go. Paul and I have to be up early."

"The night is young," Paul said. "I'm going to stay a little longer."

"Lay off the booze," Les warned. "We've got a morning boat trip."

"Don't worry," Paul said. "I'll be fine."

"Yeah right."

As Les turned to leave, Paul stuck his tongue out at him.

A glance at Danny's face told me he was as uncomfortable as I was. Weasel looked miserable. "We should go, Danny," I said. "I've got a battery charger I need to unplug. You coming, Weasel?"

Danny didn't need prodding; he waved good-bye and was halfway to the street before I finished speaking. Weasel dawdled, hoping, I think, that Laurie would ask him to stay. She didn't. He caught up with Danny and me as we headed south. We were silent till we'd put the beach bar far behind us.

"Glad I'm not going out on Paul's boat. He'll be hung over tomorrow. I wonder why Les puts up with him. He's a disaster waiting to happen," Danny remarked.

"From the look on Les' face, I don't think Paul will be with him much longer," I said.

"Les can't fire him," Weasel volunteered. "Paul is his boss."

"What?" That came from Danny.

"Van Slyke loaned Les money to rebuild North Shore Diving and became its owner when Les defaulted. Paul's dad bought the business and property from Van Slyke and made Paul the dive store's manager," Weasel explained. "Les hates having Paul as his boss but he needs the job."

A thought struck me. "Did Paul and Laurie ever date?" I asked.

"Yes," Weasel answered glumly. He refused to say more.

Chapter 12

Bonamer is noted for its great shore diving. Each of the more than 60 dive sites off its western coast has a mooring buoy in the water and a yellow rock on land that has the site's name on it in black paint. Ocean entries are easily made through gentle surf measured in inches.

Danny and I were eager to dive Bonamer's north end, rarely visited by SeaSide Inn boats because it was so far away. We also wanted to see as much as possible of the boomerang-shaped island. That meant driving south along the western coast before turning north and going through the island's interior.

Weasel wouldn't be joining us. He said beach dives were "too much work." He seemed a bit out of sorts.

For the first time since we arrived on Bonamer, we were awake before Ryan fired up the compressor. We loaded the SeaSide Inn van with dive gear, towels, T-shirts, sunscreen and a cooler filled with lunch, snacks and bottles of water.

The temperature varies little on Bonamer. It is always hot, night and day. If you want to stay cool, hot liquids are the last things you should drink; still I needed caffeine to clear the fog in my head in the morning. I had tried and been disappointed with Sara and Ryan's beverage of choice, Diet Coke. It just didn't open my eyes and jump-start my brain.

Danny didn't need coffee to wake him up, he drank it because he liked it. He and I sipped mugs of it as we drove south along the main two-lane highway. We passed a couple of large resorts, the airport, and a variety of houses and condos. We saw several of the yellow rocks that indicated dive sites. Before long, the Salt Pier came into view, stretching into the ocean. Opposite it were the evaporation not pans and, at their southern end, enormous piles of salt.

When, much like the compressor, my brain sputtered to life, I took out the Bonamer guidebook I'd bought and summarized its information for Danny as he drove. "Shallow depressions on the shore are flooded with sea water. When it evaporates, salt is left behind.

"Once a year, the salt is collected, washed and stored in piles, where it is left to dry for several months. Then it is loaded onto vessels docked at the Salt Pier via conveyor belts and shipped as far away as New Zealand."

"The pier looks like a great place to dive," Danny said. "Ryan says it's similar to the Town Pier, with lots of fish and pilings covered with sponges and corals."

"We'll have to get Laurie to take us there," I said.

Since visitors were not allowed to walk on the pier, Danny and I had fun photographing each other near it and the obelisk erected to guide ships to shore before it was built. We also photographed each other with chunks of salt. From afar, the piles looked soft and white as snow, but up close they were composed of sharp edged crystals, some of them several inches long.

A little farther south we stopped to look at the Slave Huts. Before slavery was abolished in 1862, the slaves (many Bonamer residents are their descendants) who worked the saltpans lived in small mud huts. While those that stood along the shore in two different places today were replicas, they were a chilling reminder of the inhumane way people treated other people in the not so distant past.

As we neared the southern tip of the island the ocean got noticeably rougher. Since they aren't dived very often, the reefs here are said to be some of the island's most pristine. From the way Danny reconnoitered the beach, I figured it was only a matter of time before we'd be making a surf entry here.

There were no buildings in this area. A large saltwater estuary stretched along the inland side of the road. In the distance we saw flocks of the island's signature birds, pink flamingoes. According to the guidebook, the birds built mud nests and reared their young in this sanctuary, which was off-limits to visitors. The guidebook said that eating brine shrimp in the salt ponds made the flamingos' plumage pink.

We drove on, stopping briefly to photograph a second set of

Slave Huts. Not long afterward we arrived at the Sud Punt Lighthouse. No one is allowed inside so we photographed the outside and moved on.

We'd just turned north when Danny said, "Ryan did sleep with Laurie."

It took me a moment to absorb that. "How do you know?"

"He told me while he was barbecuing the other night. I told him we were very impressed with Laurie's ability to find sea life and her knowledge of marine biology. He said a lot of customers come back year after year because of her. He keeps her on staff even though Sara wants him to fire her."

"Sara knows he slept with Laurie?"

"The whole island knows. Paul spread the news in retaliation when Ryan fired him. Ryan said it happened when Sara went to see her family in California. She was supposed to be gone two weeks; she stayed a month. He was afraid she wasn't coming back. He swears it only happened because he was drunk."

"Must be hard for Sara to see Laurie every day."

"Ryan claims he'll fire Laurie when business picks up. He regrets getting involved with her. Since he doesn't want her to suspect he's going to fire her as soon as possible, he gives her whatever she wants. She drives the newest boat and gets Sundays off."

"Laurie may be happy but Sara's not," I said. "It would help if she could dive more often but she usually gets stuck in the shop."

"Ryan should let her take the boats out more often," Danny agreed. "She's certainly capable. She'd build her own following if he'd let her."

"That marriage looks pretty shaky to me," I said.

"I know Sara wants to see her family again," Danny said. "Ryan says they can't afford it. I think he's afraid she'll stay once she gets there."

While we were talking we had come to a large, shallow bay, notable for its naturist resort. This was the island's windward side and the bay was dotted with the colorful sails of windsurfers. I put a telephoto lens on my camera and Danny got out his video. We both shot the action for a while.

Back on the road, the van took us past a small village. Then we traveled through a sparsely populated desert punctuated by divi divi trees bent sideways by the wind, low growing brush and a variety of cactuses. The ground was hard and dotted with sharp stones. Nearly every little house we passed had goats and chickens in a fenced yard. Some of the fences were made of live cactus.

I took out the guidebook and read aloud. "For centuries, donkeys and goats had free range of the island. But the goats ate native vegetation and their owners were eventually ordered to keep them in pens. Donkeys still roam free but their population has declined so precipitously that a Donkey Sanctuary was set up near the airport to care for sick and injured animals."

I opened a bottle of water, took a sip and changed the subject. "How long have Ryan and Sara been married?"

Danny thought a minute. "About six years, I think. I was invited to the wedding but couldn't go."

"You met Sara before they left California, right?"

"I've known her almost as long as Ryan has."

"Did you ever meet his first wife?"

"Once or twice," Danny answered. "They broke up shortly after he certified me."

"Any kids?"

Danny shook his head. "No. Ryan has always wanted to own a 'dive shop in paradise.' Kids weren't part of that plan. I think that's why the first wife left."

"Maybe she just got tired of his macho behavior," I said.

Danny didn't reply.

We entered Bonamer's second largest town, Poco Kabritu, established by the Spaniards in the 16th century. The guidebook said 2,000 people lived along its narrow, dusty streets. Its only notable feature was a church at the village center.

The park entrance was only a few minutes away. We paid the entrance fee, used the bathrooms (we'd been warned there weren't any in the park) and perused the exhibits in the small museum. Then we climbed back in the van and headed to the island's northernmost dive site.

It took longer — a lot longer — to get there than we expected. At the entrance we'd been given a map of the park, which showed two routes marked by yellow and green flags. We decided on the green route, which was supposed to be the shortest way to get to the west coast. Ninety-nine percent of Bonamer's named dive sites are on the west coast because the east coast is considered too rough for diving most of the time. Danny had to determine that himself.

Our first stop was at a beautiful beach where several little *palapas*, open sided structures with palm frond roofs, had been erected as shelter from the sun. The beach was only a few hundred yards long, walled on both sides by volcanic cliffs 20 to 30 feet high. Channeled toward land, the waves were big, much like those we see on California beaches. We walked north. As far as we could see, the shoreline was surf-pounded, rough-textured coral limestone.

"No wonder no one dives here," I said. "Besides the long drive, it's dangerous."

Back at the car, Danny said, "The route looks well marked and should be easy to follow. Do you want to drive or navigate?"

We both know I was born with no sense of direction, a genetic deficiency inherited from my dad. Nonetheless, since I was hot, I chose navigating, thinking if I sat quietly I'd expend less energy and stay cooler.

Danny drove back to the road marked with both green and yellow flags. It was supposed to lead us to the route marked solely by green flags. Soon the pavement ended and dirt billowed up behind us. The van's air conditioner didn't work, which had not been a problem until now because we hadn't spent a lot of time in it. However, with the windows up, the car was unbearably hot; with them down, it was unbearably hot and dusty.

Scraggly trees and low-lying brush grew so close to the sides of the road that branches sometimes scratched the van. There were lots and lots of cacti.

Adding to my lifetime confusion as to where north, south, west and east were, I found it impossible to reconcile the flags on the map with the flags we saw. It didn't help that the green and yellow routes were the same for part of the way.

The road deteriorated. Danny had to drive at a snail's pace to dodge the potholes and rocks. He didn't want to puncture a tire he'd have to patch. The ride was bone jarring.

"Do you know where we are?" Danny asked.

"Sure," I lied.

We went through an intersection decorated with a profusion of green and yellow flags. Even I realized we'd been there at least twice before.

Danny lost it. "Give me the map," he yelled.

I probably shouldn't have thrown it at him.

The van lurched to a stop and Danny grabbed the map. A cloud of dust engulfed us.

    We didn't speak as I walked around the front of the car to driver's side and Danny walked around the back to the passenger's side.

Chapter 13

We drove on with me at the wheel. Although I didn't say anything, I barely contained my glee when we passed through that flag-flying intersection yet again, this time with Danny calling the shots. Fortunately, we eventually found the coast.

We'd wasted a lot of time. It was too late to continue to the island's northernmost dive site and still make it out of the park before it closed. We settled for a beach dive at Slaughter Bay, so named, according to the guidebook, because cattle were once slaughtered there.

Danny and I weren't speaking when I parked the van. There was no shade anywhere. We opened all the doors and windows, retrieved lunch from the cooler and ate in total silence. Danny sat sideways in the driver's seat, looking at the Caribbean; I sat sideways in the passenger's seat, with a good view of the island's highest hill. It rose to 784 feet, not at all impressive to a Californian who lives at the foot of mountains several thousand feet high.

Lunch wasn't very impressive either. The ice in our foam cooler had melted and our sandwiches were floating in tepid water. Though plastic bags had kept them dry, the peanut butter filling was so warm it oozed out with every bite. Our bottled water was nearly the same temperature as the air.

We'd packed bananas and a bag of corn chips. When Danny opened the chips, the hills came alive. Rustle, rustle, rustle; we were soon surrounded by dozens of iguanas, mostly small ones about two feet long from head to tail. Danny began breaking his chips into pieces and tossing them to the reptiles saying, "Two for me, one for you."

The food brought a very large iguana out of hiding. He was a magnificent creature about four feet long, with a raccoon-striped tail and a noble, prehistoric-looking head. I wiped my hands on my tank top and got my camera out. By throwing the chips closer and closer to him, Danny drew the iguana in until it was eating out of his hand. I put my camera aside and took up Danny's video.

When Danny asked, "Ready to go diving?" I was.

Most beaches on the island were covered with coral rubble that made walking difficult. The pieces were lightweight and no two were the same size or shape. They shifted under your feet and some had sharp edges. This beach was no exception. The rubble made carting our gear to the shoreline harder than we expected. We suited up under a blistering sun.

I was never so grateful to get into the water, a cool 80°F. I didn't mind the long swim over a sandy bottom to the drop-off. We passed large areas of staghorn coral, so called because they resemble deer horns. These low lying corals provided plenty of hiding places for small creatures but their sharp, delicate branches made photography a challenge.

The drop-off was steep and the bottom out of sight in the depths. There were lots of large purple seafans, which hosted small, white, glossy shells known as flamingo tongues. There were sponges in pink, green, yellow, brown and red. Some resembled vases, others tubes, still others, trees. There were also several species of hard corals.

Danny and I went our separate ways while remaining within each other's sight. Visibility was at least 80 feet. The sun sparkled down. The trials and tribulations of our journey faded. I felt happy and peaceful.

I don't know what made me look up but as I did, a manta ray at least 12 feet wide from wingtip to wingtip swam lazily by. I turned off my strobe and raised my camera, getting one shot of the manta silhouetted by the sun. I took another of Danny trailing behind the animal, filming it as it "flew" gracefully through the water. The moment was very special; mantas are rare in Bonamer waters.

The ray was soon lost in the blue. Danny swam over to me and took his regulator out of his mouth so I could see the big grin on his face. Then he motioned toward shore.

As we walked to the van, he said, "Was that cool or was that cool?"

"That was really, really cool," I agreed. "Did you get it on video?"

"The manta passed right over my head. I got great video. How about you?"

"I have fantastic pictures of the ray silhouetted against the sun and you filming it."

Danny came close. We were wetsuit clad and dripping wet, with tanks on our backs. Still, he managed to give me a big sloppy kiss.

"You're amazing," he said.

"You're not too shabby, either," I said.

When we'd stowed our gear in the van and viewed the images we'd shot, Danny said, "We need to get out of here before the park closes. I don't want to spend the night here. There are a lot of sites outside the park on our way home."

He studied the map before we took off. Fortunately, the sun wasn't quite as hot as it had been. Unfortunately, there was just as much dust. It was drawn to our damp hair and bodies like iron filings to a magnet.

No matter. After an hour in the water, we had cooled off and were in great spirits. Now we discovered the park was full of birds, flitting here and there among the scrawny trees and thick brush. We saw several rare green and yellow lorikeets, which are found nowhere else in the world. We also spied an egret in a salt pond.

"Too bad Weasel didn't come with us," I said. "He'll be sorry he missed the manta."

"You snooze, you lose," Danny said.

"He keeps disappearing. Where do you suppose he goes?"

"I think he's seeing Laurie," Danny offered.

"Why sneak around?"

"Don't ask me, ask him."

"He's never done anything like this before," I said.

"After that night in the bar, when Laurie and Paul were drunk, he's probably embarrassed, thinks you'll think he's a fool."

"I already think that," I said, "and Weasel knows it."

Though I kept my doubts to myself, I wasn't sure Danny knew where he was going until we reached the paved part of the road again. Soon we were out of the park and through Poco Kabritu. We paused briefly at a saltwater lake to photograph flamingos as they stalked through the water on their stilt-like legs.

We stopped at the first dive site we came to that was outside the park's boundaries. While land at the southern part of the island is at sea level, the northern part features cliffs that plunge into the ocean. Water entry at this site was via a concrete staircase built into the side of the cliff.

While it took Danny two trips to get all his gear down the stairs, it took me three. I was overheated when I jumped into the water from the concrete platform at the bottom of the steps.

The sun was low on the horizon and the water was gloomy below 40 feet. We stayed shallow, cruising around leisurely. At this time of day, activity on the reef intensifies. The creatures know night is coming and the rush to find dinner and a place to sleep is on. The highlight of the dive was a school of a dozen little reef squid. Every once in a while one of them would let us get close before it jetted off. The animals changed colors rapidly: white to brown to iridescent lavender. Little fins on the sides of their bodies fluttered continuously and their large eyes checked us out.

After the dive, the trek back up the staircase seemed twice as long.

I drove the final leg of our trip. Danny said as long as I stayed on the road and didn't make any turns, we'd be okay.

Sunburned, hot and sticky with salt and dust, we craved two things: an ice-cold beer and food. Instead of going directly to the SeaSide Inn, we decided to have pizza in town. I parked in front of the mall and we pulled shorts and shirts on over our swimsuits.

In the restroom, I washed my face and tried, without success, to smooth my hair. Its natural color was obscured by dust and it stuck out all over. My nose was so sunburned it may have rivaled Rudolph's in wattage. My tank top was wrinkled and streaked with dirt. Smears of peanut butter decorated the hem. I was too hungry and thirsty to care. I took comfort in the fact that Danny wouldn't look any better.

When I came out of the restroom, I found Danny at a table with Karin Van Slyke and a fussy-looking little man. She was classy and immaculate in a black and white sundress with a tropical fish motif. The man wore a spotless white polo shirt tucked into khaki shorts. An expression of distaste flitted across his face when he looked at me.

I felt dirtier, sweatier and stickier than ever. Indeed, I was sure I'd never been this dirty, sweaty and sticky.

Danny was oblivious to our disheveled condition. There was a huge smile on his sunburned face. He'd had two great dives, was sipping an ice-cold beer and would soon be eating pizza. Life doesn't get much better for him.

"I told Karin about the manta ray," he said.

Karin said, "That's so exciting. You are extremely lucky. Most Bonamer divers have never seen one, me included.

"Cinnamon," she continued, "I'd like to introduce my dear friend Hugo van der Mer."

Hugo rose. He was several inches shorter than Karin, with a goatee and thinning hair arranged in an especially bad comb-over. I extended my right hand — it was clean, I'd just washed it — but instead of shaking it, he bowed stiffly.

"It sounds like you had a wonderful day, Cinnamon," he said in English with a heavy Dutch accent.

"It turned out great," I said. "Although when we got lost in the park I thought we'd never get out."

Danny grinned. "Cinnamon's navigationally challenged. Not that she'd ever admit it." He planted a kiss on my cheek as I sat down beside him.

"There are worse faults," Hugo said.

"Don't you dare mention any of mine," Karin implored.

"I would never reveal a lady's secrets." Hugo took Karin's left hand in his and brought it to his lips. The huge diamond on her third finger sparkled in the rays of the setting sun.

Karin saw me looking at her ring. "Isn't it beautiful? Hugo proposed last night. We're getting married."

"I knew she couldn't resist forever," Hugo gloated.

"That's terrific," Danny said. "Will you live here?"

"No. My business is in Amsterdam," Hugo said. "I have a vacation house here, though, so we will visit often."

"Won't you miss the island?" I asked Karin.

"I love Bonamer," Karin said. "It will always have a special place in my heart. It's time to leave, though. My mother is getting on in years and I have a sister and a brother in Amsterdam. I look forward to seeing them and their children more than once or twice a year."

Our pizzas arrived and the talk turned to less personal subjects. Karin asked, "Have the police learned anything new about Neils' death?"

"If they have, we wouldn't know," I said. "Westwood dropped by and demanded the video we shot when we found Van Slyke's body. We haven't seen or heard from him since."

"The island police have little experience with murder," Hugo said. "It will be a miracle if they find the killer."

Once our hunger was appeased, Danny and I headed to the SeaSide Inn. We needed a shower. We also had to rinse our gear and get our camera systems ready for the morning dive.

Weasel wasn't parked in front of the TV at our apartment. He wasn't in his room, either. "Where is he?" I asked. "Out with Laurie again?"

"He's a big boy," Danny said. "Don't worry about him."

When we were ready for bed, I asked Danny to apply a soothing cream to my sunburned back. That led to an activity that kept us awake for quite awhile. A good day of diving is an aphrodisiac to Danny. I was amazed (and pleased) by his energy level after our long day. Afterward, I fell into a deep and contented sleep.

Chapter 14

When I entered the kitchen the next morning, Weasel was on the little balcony outside, reading a book. I don't know when he got home. I didn't ask and he didn't tell.

As Danny and I worked on our camera systems, we told him about our trip to the park.

"Damn," Weasel said. "I'd like to have seen the manta."

"How were your dives?" I asked. "Anything exciting?"

"Didn't dive," Weasel answered.

"Why?" I asked.

"Didn't feel like it," Weasel said.

"What did you do?" I persisted.

"Whoa, Cinnamon," Danny interjected. "If he wants you to know, he'll tell you."

Weasel threw Danny a grateful look. "Gotta get ready for the dive," he mumbled as he fled to his room.

"I don't care if you're seeing Laurie," I called after him. He paused for a second but didn't turn around.

The three of us buddied up for the morning dive off Ryan's boat. It was relaxing and fun.

Although he dived with us, Weasel chose to sit where I couldn't talk to him on the boat. I made a mental note to stop prying into his affairs. Danny was right; if he wanted us to know, he'd tell us.

We all went out on Laurie's boat in the afternoon. It was interesting to watch her and Weasel studiously ignore each other.

Avoiding both Laurie and me put Weasel in a quandary. The boat wasn't that big. I watched the confusion on his expressive face as he tried to figure out where to sit just before the boat left the dock. He eventually plunked himself down between a man and his wife, forcing them to scoot over to make room for him and ignoring the glares he got from them. I quickly changed places with Danny so when Weasel looked up, I was right across from him. I grinned and he turned beet red.

"Shame on you," Danny whispered in my ear. He, however, couldn't suppress a smile.

Danny, Weasel and I had requested the island's southernmost dive site, Red Slave Huts, visited infrequently because it's so far away. Everyone thought that was a good idea so that's where we headed.

The boat ride was relatively smooth. I took that opportunity to chat with Laurie as she drove the boat. Although she could describe the lives of little sea creatures in great detail, she was guarded about her own.

"How did you learn to speak English so well?"

"My dad's American."

"How did your parents meet?"

"He was stationed in Germany for several years."

"Did you grow up there?"

"I was born in Germany but I've lived all over the place."

"Where are your parents now?"

"My dad lives in the Oregon, my mother's in Munich."

"How long have you been here?"

"Five years."

"Why did you come to Bonamer?"

"Like everyone else, to dive."

Laurie kept her eyes on the sea in front of her, never glancing my way. The conversation was too much work. I went back to my seat.

Near the south end of the island, the ride got bumpy. The water was choppy at the mooring buoy. I saw apprehension in Weasel's eyes, but he didn't say anything. Since none of us had been to this site before, Laurie suggested we make a group dive with her as the leader. We gathered around the mooring buoy anchor to wait for Laurie, who had to help everyone else get into the water before she joined us. When she descended and swam toward the drop-off, seven people trailed along behind her.

Underwater it was calm, with a mild current. The site was beautiful. The reef looked pristine and was full of feathery brown and green soft corals three to five feet tall. In one sandy clearing a five-foot long barracuda hung overhead. While Danny and I know these silvery fish pose no threat to divers, Weasel cast several anxious looks at it and stuck close to us.

Laurie found lots of little creatures, including a bright yellow seahorse. We saw four turtles swim by, one of which was missing a rear flipper. When I pointed it out to Danny, he pantomimed "shark" with an unmistakable gesture. From then on, Weasel was never more than a few inches from Danny or me. He was so close he kept bumping into us.

We ascended to find the ocean's surface had gotten rougher and a current had sprung up. Swimming to the boat and climbing into it were difficult. The trip to the SeaSide Inn was very bumpy; we were drenched with spray continuously. We didn't bother to take off our wetsuits; we were warmer with them on. A couple of people even wore dive masks to keep saltwater out of their eyes.

We returned to the SeaSide Inn much later than usual. Ryan's boat was already at the dock, its passengers long gone.

Ryan ran down the pier to help Laurie tie up our boat and she tossed a line to him. As he wound it around a cleat, Westwood and another police officer strode toward us. I thought I saw a flicker of trepidation on Ryan's face as he grabbed a second line and secured the boat. The divers began unloading their gear and scrambling off.

Ryan straightened up, folded his arms across his chest and faced the policemen. "What can I do for you?"

"Come to the station," Westwood said. "We need to talk to you and your wife."

"We can't go right now," Ryan said. "We've got tanks to fill and customers to help."

Westwood bristled. "You will come with us now. We'll use handcuffs if we have to."

Ryan looked as if he'd been punched in the stomach. The officers escorted him to the dive store and they all went inside.

Laurie hurried after them but the door was locked and she couldn't get in.

Danny, Weasel and I also headed toward the dive shop. The door opened as we reached it and Ryan and Sara came out, followed by the policemen. None of them looked at or spoke to us as they got into the patrol car parked in the driveway. I'll never forget seeing Sara's stricken face as they drove off. She looked as if her world had ended.

Laurie, Danny, Weasel and I just stood there, dumfounded.

"Bonamer cops have a very unorthodox way of doing things," I said. "They cart our friends off to jail, but have yet to search the SeaSide Inn for evidence. This is not the way criminal investigations are conducted in America."

"This isn't America," Laurie pointed out. "What am I going to do? I can't run this place by myself."

"Cinnamon and I will help," Danny said.

"Me, too," Weasel piped up.

Just then several SeaSide Inn guests gathered around us to ask what had happened. I thought Laurie handled the situation very well.

"I don't know any more than you do," she told them. "I hope Ryan and Sara won't be gone long. In the meantime, I'll do everything I can to keep the SeaSide Inn running as usual."

A few minutes later, she, Danny, Weasel and I huddled in Ryan's tiny office, a separate room at the back of the dive store.

"I'm a dive shop owner and an instructor," Danny said. "I've been working on boats since I was in high school and have my captain's license. I could run Ryan's boat."

Laurie looked at him and I could see her assessing his abilities. "I'll need to check out your boat handling skills. We can do that before I leave tonight. If you pass my test, I'll give you a book Ryan put together. It lists all the dive sites and has all the information you'll need to know about each one of them."

"Weasel and I can take care of the store," I said. "We work the sales floor in my Dad's place."

"You don't know our inventory or procedures," Laurie said. "Can you sell regulators and dive computers?"

"They're both quick studies," Danny said. "The shop isn't that big and it isn't that busy. It won't be long before they know every inch of it."

Laurie looked doubtful.

"What have you got to lose?" Danny asked. "We're free and available."

"Okay," Laurie said. "We'll give it a try. Right now the tanks from my boat need to be unloaded and filled."

"We're on it," Danny said. He and Weasel went back to the boat. Before long I heard the clang of tanks and the tank dolly rolling up the pier. A few minutes later, the compressor started up.

Laurie and I went into the dive shop, where several guests had gathered. I sold T-shirts, batteries for a dive computer and a couple of marine life identification books. Laurie checked in rental gear and prepared bills for those who were going home the next day. After all the customers left, she went over some of the things I'd need to know.

Danny and Weasel came in before she finished. "Are the tanks out for the night divers?" Laurie asked.

"Yep," Danny said. "We filled all of the tanks and closed the compressor room. It's ready to be locked."

"If Ryan and Sara don't come back tonight I'll need you to fill any tanks used by night divers and load all of the tanks onto the boats tomorrow morning."

"We'll be ready," Danny said.

"Let's see how you handle a boat," Laurie said.

Weasel and I went to our apartment and, from the balcony overlooking the Caribbean, watched as Laurie put Danny through the paces.

From our vantage point, Danny's performance was perfect. Laurie seemed pleased; she smiled and clapped him on the shoulder when he stepped off onto the pier.

Danny returned to the apartment pleased with his success and we took a shower together. When we finished, Weasel and his laptop were gone. I looked for him on the pool deck, where I thought he'd be checking his e-mails, but he wasn't there.

Knowing we might have to work the next day, Danny and I made a night dive off the pier in front of the SeaSide Inn. Four other guests had the same idea. It was an entertaining, pleasant dive and would have been the perfect ending to another perfect day if Ryan and Sara were safely at home instead of in the Bonamer jail.

The door to Weasel's bedroom was closed when we got back to our apartment so I assumed he'd gone to bed early. Camera maintenance consumed the rest of our evening.

For the first time since our arrival on Bonamer, Danny set the alarm clock. He wanted to be ready to fire up the compressor in the morning if Ryan wasn't around.

Chapter 15

Sara fought panic. She'd told the police she was claustrophobic, as had Ryan. Still, they locked her in a tiny cell with a concrete floor and three solid walls. One side had bars so at least she could see out. That helped, but didn't eliminate her problem entirely.

Sara felt the walls closing in on her. She didn't want to be here, couldn't stand to be here. Sweat popped out on her forehead and her heart beat faster and faster.

It was all Karin's fault. When she called and asked for help, Sara had to say yes. She and Paul had been meeting in Karin's condo for several weeks.

Karin had been stressed, really, really stressed. Almost as stressed as Sara was now, locked in this minuscule cell. Sara could still remember that call, word for word.

"You have to help me. Neils collapsed and died in my bedroom several minutes ago. I think he had a heart attack.

"Hugo will be arriving on the island in a couple of hours. I need Neils out of here," Karin's voice broke. "You have to help me, I can't do it alone, he's too heavy."

Sara didn't want anything to do with a dead body but what choice did she have? Still, she tried to wiggle out of the task.

"Are you sure he's dead?"

"What kind of a lunatic do you think I am? Of course he's dead." Karin was impatient.

"Can't you call an ambulance?"

"You know I can't," Karin had said. "No one must find out I was still seeing Neils."

Sara had driven to Karin's place reluctantly, telling Ryan she had an errand to do. Absorbed in a baseball game on TV, his response was automatic and unintelligible.

Neils turned out to be nearly too much even for the two of them. They had to get him out of the bed on the second floor and down the stairs to the first floor. He was a big man and his limp, weighty body was extraordinarily hard to handle. Both women were soon perspiring profusely.

Sara pulled her car into Karin's garage and closed the door. Somehow the women managed to hoist Neils' sheet shrouded body into the trunk.

"What do I do now?" Sara dabbed at the sweat on her forehead with a tissue.

"I don't care," Karin said. "Just get him out of here. I have to change the linens, shower and pick up Hugo."

"I can't possibly lift him out of the trunk by myself," Sara said.

"Leave him in there, then," Karin said. "We'll figure out what to do about him tomorrow."

"Leave a dead man in my trunk overnight? No, no, no!" Sara protested, her voice rising.

"Then ask Ryan for help. I'm sure he'll have some good ideas. Now go. I don't have much time."

Driving home, Sara freaked out. It was only a couple of miles and she knew there was zero chance any Bonamer cop would pull her over. Still, she worried. An accident would be disastrous. She drove the speed limit, was super careful about using the turn signal and checked her rear view mirror constantly.

She parked in the garage and went to tell Ryan she had the body of a man he despised in her car.

He took the news remarkably well. To Sara's surprise, he quickly devised a plan to dispose of the dead man. While Sara did not like it and said so, Ryan would not budge. She had to go along with his plan or leave Neils in her trunk, which was just too horrible to contemplate.

Ryan's plan, however, was more challenging than they'd anticipated. At one point Sara had a chance to change it and acted on her impulse. All she wanted was for the body to be out of their boat. What she did, however, made things worse. The police knew the body had been moved — twice — and were determined to find out who had done it and why. Ryan kept assuring Sara they hadn't done anything illegal. Yet here they were, in jail.

Sara glanced wildly around her enclosure. A wave of nausea hit her and she felt lightheaded and dizzy. Karin must know where they were, the whole island would know by now. Why wasn't Karin here, telling the police how Neils had died so they could go home?

For the first time, a thought buried deep in Sara's subconscious surfaced. What if Neils' death wasn't natural? What if Karin had killed him? What if Sara had to spend the rest of her life in a tiny, tiny cell?

Sara couldn't hold back the panic any longer. She began to scream.

Chapter 16

Danny, who usually slept soundly, didn't. I know that because I, too, had a restless night. Both of us were up well before the alarm went off. In the morning quiet we sat on the sofa in the living room, drinking coffee and discussing the stunning events of the previous night.

"Ryan was afraid the police would think he killed Van Slyke when they saw that concrete cylinder," Danny said. "Guess he was right. But why did they arrest Sara?"

"They probably think she's the weakest link, that she'll break down and tell them what they want to know. I think that's a good guess. She's claustrophobic and won't like being in a cell."

"Ryan can be a jerk sometimes but a killer? No way," Danny said.

"I agree," I said. "And he's too smart to use a concrete cylinder from his own fence and put a No Tees hat on the body. Someone set him up."

Weasel appeared in the doorway, a cup of coffee in one hand. From the looks of him, he hadn't slept well either. As he sat down he asked, "What are we going to do?"

"Run the resort and try to keep the guests happy," Danny said.

"If the Millers aren't back by lunchtime, I'll go see Westwood at the jail," I said. "Find out how long he expects to hold them. Maybe he'll even let me talk to them."

There was silence as we sipped our coffee. Weasel volunteered: "I'm not sleeping with Laurie. I've been taking a divemaster course from her."

Danny's eyebrows shot up. "What?"

My mouth dropped open and I stared at Weasel for several long minutes as I processed his news.

"Why keep it a secret?" I asked when I found my voice.

Weasel shifted uneasily. "It's not a SeaSide Inn course, Laurie's moonlighting. Besides, I wanted to surprise you."

"You've certainly done that. However, it's wrong to cheat Ryan out of money for a course one of his instructors is teaching. Did you forget we're staying here for free?" Danny was upset.

Weasel hung his head. "It was cheaper. And Laurie said Ryan wouldn't care as long as Sara didn't find out. Besides, as I said, it was supposed to be a surprise. I was going to tell you when I'd passed the exam. Only now it doesn't look like I'll be able to complete the class work."

"What happened?" I asked.

"Lots of stuff. Remember that night you joined us in the bar? We were just going to have a quick drink before class. Then Les and Paul showed up. You know what happened next.

"We were supposed to have a class last night. Laurie told me to meet her at the bar, then was two hours late. She said she was too upset about Ryan and Sara to teach."

"Cancel the class and ask for your money back," Danny said. "You can finish it at home with me."

"I tried. Laurie said she'd already spent the money and besides, we could make up the classes on her day off. If she gets one, that is."

Danny glanced at the clock. "Time to go to work."

We trooped downstairs. Laurie had already opened the dive store. Danny fired up the compressor. The morning routine had begun.

An hour later, the two boats departed, with Danny running one and Laurie the other.

Weasel and I staffed the dive store, which was pretty quiet when most of the resort's guests were out on the boats. We used the time to acquaint ourselves with the merchandise and I taught a gloomy Weasel what I had learned from Laurie the previous evening.

A couple of hours passed. No customers came in and Weasel wasn't inclined to be chatty. I left him sitting on a stool reading a marine life ID book and went back to our apartment to get his laptop. On a chaise lounge near the pool, I accessed my e-mail and updated Dad on what had been happening on Bonamer.

At the dive store afterward, I called the police station. I asked for Officer Westwood and was told he wasn't available. I asked to

---

speak to Ryan and Sara and was told that only family members or their lawyer could talk to them. Finally, I asked if I could visit them. The answer, of course, was another no.

"I can handle things here," Weasel said. "Why don't you just go down there?"

I walked to town. The results were the same. No Westwood, no speaking to or visiting the Millers. I did learn they could be held up to 48 hours without any charges being filed and a judge could extend that time if he felt it was justified. That made things worse. Danny, Weasel and I had to go home in few days. Laurie would to have to find help, and find it quickly, if the SeaSide Inn was to survive.

"Do the Millers have a lawyer?" I asked.

"Yes," the officer behind the counter said.

Amazingly, he gave me the lawyer's name, address and phone number. The man's office was in the town mall, only a few minutes away. When I got there, however, the door was locked and no one answered my knock. Thoroughly frustrated, I went back to the SeaSide Inn.

Danny's boat returned no more than five minutes later and Laurie's came in shortly thereafter. There was no time to tell anyone what I'd learned because we were all very busy for the next hour.

At noon, Laurie locked the dive store and went into Ryan's office to have lunch. Danny, Weasel and I went to our place and had our midday meal on the oceanside balcony.

"How did it go?" I asked Danny.

"Great," he said. "We went to Divi Divi Tree. That's where we saw that big green moray two days ago."

I told Danny and Weasel about my visit to the police station and the lawyer's office. "I'll call him this afternoon."

"The 48 hours will be up tomorrow afternoon," Danny said. "But I hope they'll let Ryan and Sara come home before then."

"Me, too," Weasel said.

"Me three," I said. "Why don't you dive this afternoon, Weasel? The store doesn't need two people. We can alternate."

"Good idea," Danny said. "That way each of you can make at least one dive every day."

Once again, when the boats departed, everything quieted down. I called the lawyer and got his voice mail. I said I was a friend of the Millers and wanted to talk to him. Since there was no phone in our apartment, I left the dive store number and the hours it was open.

I also called the police station. I was astonished when Westwood came on the line.

"Danny and I really need to talk to Ryan and Sara," I said. "We have questions about the business."

"Ask Laurie," Westwood told me. "She's been at the SeaSide Inn longer than they have."

"Will the Millers be released tomorrow?"

"Hard to tell," Westwood said. "Our investigation is not complete. I do have some questions for you, though. Can you come talk to me now?"

"I'm the only one in the dive store," I said. "I'd have to close it."

"Ah well, too bad," Westwood said. "What you tell us might get your friends out of jail."

Damn. Was that just a ploy to get me down there? What if it wasn't? "I'll be there in 10 minutes," I said. I locked the door to the little store and turned the card in the window to the side that read "Closed."

At the station, the officer at the front desk notified Westwood. The station was hot, calm and, except for the sound of the fan whirling overhead, very quiet.

Westwood led me down a hall to a small, neat office in the back of the building. Cooled by a fan on the top of a file cabinet, its furnishings were sparse and inexpensive. Westwood seemed more relaxed than he'd been the other times I'd seen him. He sat in the chair behind a nondescript desk and motioned me to a chair in front of it.

"Do you mind if I video this?" he asked.

"Uhm, no," I said. Filming interviews was standard operating procedure at Cliffview PD. "Where is the camera?"

Westwood pointed to a tiny camera mounted near the ceiling in a corner of the room.

"Is this your first visit to Bonamer?" Westwood asked.

"Yes."

"How long have you known Ryan and Sara Miller?"

"I met them when we arrived on Bonamer. Danny has known them longer. Ryan taught him to dive."

"So the Millers and your boyfriend are close personal friends?" Westwood seemed to be inferring that Danny and the Millers were long-time partners in crime.

"Danny and Ryan worked at the same California dive store. They saw a lot of each other then. Since the Millers moved to Bonamer three years ago, Danny's only contact with Ryan has been via e-mail."

"Your crime scene footage is very good," Westwood said, changing the subject. "Have you had professional training?"

"I work part-time as a forensic photographer for the Cliffview Police Department," I said.

"You are a police officer?"

"No, I'm a civilian employee." I got the feeling Westwood already knew the answers to his questions.

Westwood continued. "While your video has been very helpful, we wish you had mentioned it the night Van Slyke was found."

Westwood was right about the video being helpful. The Millers were in jail because of it — because of me. That was upsetting.

"There was so much going on," I said. "We were shocked the body was gone when we tried to take you to it. We forgot all about the video until we were back at the SeaSide Inn. We intended to give you a copy the next morning but got sidetracked.

"Anyone could have stolen that concrete cylinder," I went on. "It was on the beach, right in front of the Millers' house. And what better way to point a finger at Ryan than to put a No Tees hat on the body?"

"It could also be a clever way to make the Bonamer police think he was being set up," Westwood said.

I didn't like the way things were going. I shouldn't have come to the police station. I stood up. "I have to go. No one is minding the dive store."

"Just a couple more questions," Westwood said.

"Not unless you answer one of mine," I said. "I know there's been an autopsy. What caused Van Slyke's death?"

"I can't tell you that," Westwood answered. "It might compromise our investigation."

I turned and walked out.

As I got in the van, I pondered my stupidity. My visit with Westwood hadn't done anyone any good. I looked at my watch. I'd been gone less than 20 minutes. If I got back before I was missed, I wouldn't have to mention this fiasco to anyone.

The boats were still out and the store was just as I left it. I breathed a sigh of relief and settled onto the stool behind the counter.

Chapter 17

I wasn't alone in the shop for long. To my dismay, Westwood showed up about ten minutes later.

"I don't want to talk to you," I said.

"We got off on the wrong foot," he said. "I apologize. I only wanted to chat with you. An exchange of information, if you will."

"You're trying to make me incriminate my friends."

"We won't even mention them. Let me ask you why you think Van Slyke was killed."

"He was a ruthless, greedy man who wanted to build a golf course that would pollute the water and eventually put dive operators out of business," I said. "Ryan and Sara aren't the only ones who didn't like him. He had lots of enemies. Why don't you check out some of them?"

"The Millers told you Van Slyke was an evil man?"

"Yes."

"Your friends dwell on the negatives," Westwood said, "and ignore the positives."

"I didn't think there were any."

"Van Slyke was known for his philanthropy. He was one of the primary benefactors of the Donkey Sanctuary and spearheaded the drive to buy Little Bonamer and turn it into a park so it would never be developed. He also donated money to construct a new building for our hyperbaric chamber. It is used, as I am sure you know, to treat dive accidents."

"That may be true," I said. "But he sold Les Gudrow's land right out from under him and divorced Karin, leaving her with next to nothing, so he could marry a younger woman."

"Les usually neglects to mention that his dive store was

destroyed by storm surge two different times yet he rebuilt on the exact same spot," Westwood said. "He was unable to get insurance after the second time. When the store was washed away the third time, Van Slyke loaned him the money to rebuild but took the deed to the land as collateral. Gudrow was supposed to start repaying the loan after a year. When he defaulted on the payments Van Slyke foreclosed."

Westwood wasn't finished. "There are widespread rumors about how poorly Karin fared in her divorce. Those are rumors she started and nurtured over the years. They aren't true. I have seen a copy of their prenup and it was quite generous."

"Why would she make false claims? And why wouldn't he refute them?" I asked.

Westwood shrugged. "I can only guess. As Neils' wife, Karin got used to lavish spending. She did not become thrifty when she got divorced. A lot of money went into her boutique, which has always operated in the red. Maybe the rumors were intended to goad Neils into giving her even more money.

"Karin's mother begged her to be civil to Neils. This is a small island. They had many mutual friends. He owned the Green Iguana and had an office there, so they ran into each other all the time."

I said: "I heard Neils didn't want children when he and Karin were married. Yet he had two children with his second wife."

"It is true that Neils remarried as soon as the divorce was final and his new wife was already pregnant.

"However, having children hasn't been an option for Karin for decades. She had problems that resulted in a complete hysterectomy when she was 18."

"How do you know all of this?" I asked.

"Van Slyke's philanthropic activities are easily verified by the organizations that benefited from them. A little research was necessary to document Les' problems.

"I know about Karin, more than I would like to, actually, because when her mother comes to Bonamer for extended visits she plays bridge with my Dutch grandmother and her cronies. Those old ladies know everybody's business."

"Surely you wouldn't base a murder investigation on gossip," I protested.

"Of course not. Not all of what my grandmother hears is true," Westwood said. "Often, however, where there is smoke, there is fire.

The terms of the divorce are in a legal document and I have a copy."

I absorbed what Westwood had told me. "You have a Dutch grandmother?" I asked.

Westwood raised an eyebrow. "Yes. I'm half Dutch, half American. My mother was born in Amsterdam, my father in San Francisco. They owned a restaurant here for many years. They sold it and moved to Pasadena when I was in junior high."

I was speechless for a few minutes. "You grew up in California? How on earth did you become a cop here?"

Westwood didn't answer right away. Finally he said: "I spent six years with the LAPD. I loved my job until I had an encounter with a carjacker. Several of us chased him all over the city for nearly two hours. We finally cornered him and ordered him out of the SUV he stole. He came out firing a small handgun we didn't know he had. We had no choice but to return fire. The carjacker and his baby daughter, who was asleep in the backseat, were killed.

"We didn't know there was anyone else in the car. We were devastated. Still, the public and the media labeled us child killers.

"Even though everyone involved was eventually absolved of blame, that incident destroyed our lives. My partner fired the shot that killed the baby. He committed suicide on the first anniversary of her death. I came to Bonamer where there are no high-speed pursuits or shootouts with criminals."

"Why are you telling me all this?" I asked.

"I believe you and your friends know more about Van Slyke's death than you have admitted," Westwood said. "I have been honest and forthcoming with you. I hope you will be the same with me."

"We didn't know Van Slyke when he was alive," I said. "We have no idea who killed him, though we're absolutely positive it wasn't Ryan or Sara. And you haven't been that forthcoming. How did Van Slyke die?"

"I can't tell you that.

"I think you will find out, perhaps accidentally, who was involved in Van Slyke's death. I am only asking you to let me know if and when you learn anything."

"You're asking me to spy on my friends. I won't do that."

"I talked to the Chief of the Cliffview Police," Westwood said calmly. "He said you can be stubborn and difficult to work with but you always do the right thing.

"You know where to find me."

78

Westwood turned and walked out.

Chapter 18

Speechless, I sat on my stool behind the counter and watched Westwood leave. The bell on the door tinkled as he opened and closed it.

He'd made me an informant against my will.

I didn't have much time to think about that because both boats returned. For the next 45 minutes the shop was filled with people buying things, signing up for Laurie's classes and looking through the used paperback novels left by previous guests. They were available for free if you left one in trade.

When the last customer departed, Laurie and I went out to the boat sign-up board to discuss the next day's schedule with Danny and Weasel.

A patrol car pulled up in the driveway. Conversation stopped. The back doors of the car opened and Ryan and Sara stepped out. The car drove off.

Ryan's face mirrored the severe strain he was under and Sara's eyes were teary. We welcomed them back with hugs.

"Are you out for good?" I asked.

Ryan shrugged. "We don't know. They won't tell us anything."

"How are you?" I asked Sara.

"Okay. Glad to be out of that little cell."

"We've got cold beer, want to celebrate with a couple at our place?" Danny asked.

"Sara and I really need some quiet time together right now," Ryan said. He draped an arm around his wife's shoulders. "Can we have a rain check?"

I glanced at Laurie as Ryan opened the gate to their yard and ushered Sara through it. Her face wore an odd expression, one I couldn't read.

Although the Millers didn't want to celebrate, Danny, Weasel and I did. A load had been lifted from our collective shoulders; we'd gotten our vacations back.

"Let's go someplace nice for dinner," Weasel said. "My treat."

We looked at him. In all the years I've known him, Weasel has never picked up the tab for anything. Up till now, the three of us had always split the cost of our meals three ways.

"Can you afford it?" I asked.

Weasel shrugged. "Sure."

We'd heard other SeaSide divers rave about Cosima, an upscale Italian restaurant a few minutes south of the inn. We showered, put on our best clothes (a sundress for me, clean polo shirts and shorts for the guys), and walked there. Cosima operated out of a remodeled house right on the beach. Inside, potted plants and gleaming tile floors made it very pleasant. We arrived just after the restaurant opened and there were plenty of empty tables. We were ushered to one with a great view of the Caribbean Sea and the sun, now making its way toward the horizon.

Weasel ordered wine and appetizers while we studied the menu. I would have settled for the cheapest dish but Weasel ordered the most expensive. Danny followed suit. I threw frugality to the wind and made it three.

In between bites of antipasti and sips of wine I said: "You've never worked fulltime since I've known you, Weasel, but you always seem to have enough money. Where does it come from?"

Weasel blinked.

"Cinnamon," Danny said. "Your father would be horrified by your rudeness."

"My father raised me," I countered. "I am what I am because of him. He would be amazed by my audacity. He would not be horrified."

"She's right," Weasel said.

"Don't encourage her," Danny said.

"Don't prevaricate, Weasel. Tell us the source of your vast wealth."

"It's a trust fund," Weasel admitted.

"A trust fund?" I was amazed. I was joking when I mentioned "vast wealth," I hadn't expected it to be true. "From whom?"

"My great-grandfather."

"How did he acquire his fortune?"

"He was in the fashion industry."

"Doing what?"

Weasel squirmed before admitting: "He was the founder of Lucy's Lovely Lingerie."

An image of the company's famous ad, a drawing of a beautiful young blond wearing a lacy bra and matching panties, popped into my head along with the company's slogan, which I quoted: "'The Secret to a Heavenly Body.' You're kidding, right?"

"Believe me, I wouldn't kid about that."

"Are your parents still alive?"

"No. My dad died when I was in high school. My mom died a dozen years ago. You and Ted came to the funeral."

I thought a minute. "Your parents have a crypt at Forest Lawn."

"Yes," Weasel said. He was pleased I remembered.

"So, are you insanely rich?" I asked.

"Don't let her bully you," Danny advised.

"Ha! It's impossible to stop her. Surely you've discovered that," Weasel said. "If she wants to know something you *will* eventually tell her.

"Yes, there's a lot of money. Right now I get an allowance. Until I fulfill certain requirements, that's all I'll get. My parents didn't want me to drift through life spending money earned by someone else."

"You've gone back to school to get your degree so you can become gainfully employed."

Weasel nodded.

"You've seemed quite content all these years living on the allowance. What inspired the change?"

Weasel turned bright red.

"There's a woman involved, isn't there? That's why you took up diving."

Weasel wouldn't look at me. "There was a woman," he admitted. "It didn't work out."

"Anyone I know?"

Weasel met my eyes defiantly. "No."

Now I felt bad. "Sorry. That was none of my business."

"No kidding," Danny said dryly.

There were several minutes of silence. Danny broke it. "What should we do tomorrow? We don't have to work."

We drank a toast to our freedom, followed hastily by a toast to Ryan and Sara's freedom.

We walked home in the dark on the two-lane road with me in the middle. I put an arm around each of the guys. "Look at us," I said. "The Three Musketeers. Ready to fight for Peace, Justice and the American Way."

"That's Superman's mantra," Danny said.

"The Musketeers were French, not American," Weasel pointed out.

"All for one and one for all," I remembered. "That could be our motto, too."

"I agree," Danny said.

"Me, too," Weasel said.

When we got back to our apartment, Danny and I took turns editing photos and video on Weasel's laptop at the kitchen table while Weasel turned on the TV and settled down on the sofa to watch a Dodgers game.

Later, when Danny and I were in bed, I asked, "Do you think I'm too nosey?"

Even in the dark I could tell Danny was rolling his eyes.

"I'd still like to know who made Weasel decide to finish his education after all these years," I said. "She must really be something."

"You have no idea," Danny said. He chuckled.

I bolted upright. "You know who she is?"

"Think about it," Danny advised. "Weasel could have finished his education in the LA area. Instead, he attends Windgate and lives in Cliffview. He took up scuba diving and works in your dad's store."

"So?" I said. "Who is she?"

Danny sighed. "You can be such a dunce sometimes, Sunshine. Do I have to spell it out for you? What's the common link?"

The light dawned. "There's only one," I said slowly. Me."

"Bingo," Danny said. "Good night, Sunshine."

Chapter 19

The compressor: How sweet it sounded when someone else was running it and we didn't have to go to work, we got to go diving instead.

Unfortunately, none of us had remembered to sign up for a morning boat and they were full.

We found Ryan ferrying tanks down to the dock. Laurie usually helped him but she was busy in the dive store, so Danny and I volunteered. As we handed tanks to Ryan, who was standing in his boat, Danny asked if we could borrow the van for a beach dive.

"You guys don't even have to ask. Anything I have is yours. Sara has the keys."

We helped send the boats off before returning to our apartment. Weasel was in the kitchen, pouring a cup of coffee.

Danny picked up Ryan's book on dive sites and leafed through it. After awhile he asked: "Why don't we try Something Special? I've heard it's terrific. Before the marina was built it was an anchorage and boats dumped their trash there. Ryan's book says, "Expect old tires and other junk on the bottom that provide hiding places for a lot of unusual little critters. You'll also find the wreck of a small boat."

Not having a schedule was liberating. We took our time getting ready. Weasel provided a recap of the Dodgers game he'd watched on TV the previous evening. Since all of us are avid fans, there was a heated discussion of the team's season over breakfast.

While we talked, I took a good, long look at Weasel, possibly my first. When I met him, I'd been dazzled by Ted and when he came back into my life, my heart belonged to Danny.

Now it came as a revelation that he was cute. A smidge under six feet, he had short, dark brown hair, hazel eyes, a good nose and straight white teeth. I'd always thought he was out of shape and overweight. Now I noticed that somewhere along the line he'd dropped about 25 pounds and there was muscle where there used to be fat.

While Weasel had dated sporadically he'd never had a long-term girlfriend since I'd known him. Maybe women, me among them, didn't think he'd ever amount to anything. A couch potato and chronic underachiever, he wasn't known for his business acumen. He'd bought a racehorse (cheap) that turned out to be old and lame; invested in a dot.com that went bust; and been part owner of a supposedly trendy bar that went bankrupt. His nickname, coined by Ted when they were in junior high, fit him perfectly when it was bestowed. Maybe it wasn't so apt now. Come to think of it, I didn't even know his given name.

I seized a lull in the baseball discussion. "What's your full name?"

Weasel nearly choked on a mouthful of cereal. When he recovered he said, "Christopher Andrew Richardson. Why are you asking now, after all these years?"

"Anybody ever call you Chris?"

"My mom."

"Do you mind being called Weasel?"

The spoon paused just in front of Christopher Andrew Richardson's mouth and he shook his head. "Ted gave me that nickname and he's my best friend."

After breakfast, we loaded tanks, cameras and scuba gear into the van, along with bottled water and towels. It was already in the high 80s and would only get warmer.

Something Special was about 15 minutes north of the SeaSide Inn, just off the main road that ran along the coast. Accessed via a narrow dirt road between two houses, the dive site was on the south side of a channel that led to a small marina. On the north side there was a large, upscale resort.

A huge yacht was tied up on the south side of the channel. The *California Girl* was gorgeous, with three decks and a shiny white hull trimmed in blue. The railings were stainless steel, the windows (no traditional portholes on this boat), smoked glass. We stopped briefly to admire her as we lugged scuba and camera gear past her to the beach.

"How big is your trust, Weasel?" I asked. "Can you buy one of these?"

"Maybe."

We assembled BCs, regulators and tanks. When Weasel turned on his tank valve, there was a loud hiss. Danny was there in a flash, turning off the valve and removing the regulator. "You've lost an O-ring," he said. "Do you have a spare?"

Weasel looked at him blankly. "Me?"

Danny raised his eyebrows. "Cinnamon?"

"You're king of the spare parts, Mr. Instructor," I said. "Why should we carry extras when you have three of everything?"

"I usually do," Danny agreed. "Not this time. I gave my last O-ring to a guy on my boat yesterday. Guess I'd better run back to the SeaSide Inn and get one. You guys can wait here."

"Sit in the hot sun? No thanks," I said. "I'd be a crispy critter by the time you got back. Why don't we see if Les Gudrow has any? I think North Shore Diving is just up the road. I'll go with you." I turned to Weasel. "You want to come or stay here with the gear?"

"I'll stay," Weasel said. "Do you have any sunscreen?"

I tossed him a tube of SPF 50 and accompanied Danny to the van.

I'd heard that North Shore was the oldest resort on Bonamer; I hadn't heard it was out of business and rundown. Six two-story buildings sprawled across a massive property that was rapidly reverting to its natural state. The weeds were tall and brown. Paint peeled from the buildings and every window was broken.

A sign at the highway read "North Shore Diving" and had an arrow pointing west. Danny drove along the short dusty road to the beach, where we found a store that must have been cobbled together from the remains of its two predecessors. Fifty yards from the water, it sat near the base of a long pier, where a seen-better-days dive boat was tied up.

There was a rusty Jeep knock-off in the dirt parking lot and space for four more vehicles. Danny parked the van and we got out.

Inside, the tiny store was hot and smelled of mildew. It had a concrete floor and a wooden counter cleverly constructed from parts of several boats.

The compressor was running and Les was filling a tank. He wore red swim trunks and flip-flops. He was in very good shape for a man his age. He acknowledged us and mouthed, "Be right with you." We wouldn't be able to talk until he turned off the noisy machine.

That gave us time to look around. Several faded BCs and shorty wetsuits hung from a rack. I figured they were rentals.

There were a few new masks, snorkels and fins for sale and a small four-sided bookcase that held tomes on marine life and Bonamer history. Next to the bookcase, a sturdy wooden stand held a Plexiglas box with an large brass padlock. Inside was a copy of Jacques-Yves Cousteau's first book, *The Silent World.*

Scuba divers revere Cousteau, who is considered the father of our sport. He was a French naval officer in 1943 when he and industrial engineer, Emil Gagnan, invented the first successful Self-Contained Underwater Breathing Apparatus (SCUBA), which they called the Aqua-Lung. The prolific, multi-talented Cousteau made the most of his 87 years, founding the Cousteau Society and exploring the underwater world on the *Calypso* and *Alcyon* while making movies and TV specials about his adventures. *The Silent World* was the first of an extraordinary number of books with his name on them. The famous captain, often photographed wearing a red wool watch cap, died in 1997.

I knew all this because Danny gave a talk about diving history to each and every one of his classes, usually in the galley of a boat in between the dives leading to their certification. I'd heard this talk so often I could recite it from memory.

Les finished filling the tank and turned off the compressor.

"Is this a first edition?" I indicated the book. I'm not sure why I asked, I know absolutely nothing about first editions or what makes a book valuable.

"You betcha," Les said. "Published in 1953. My dad gave it to me for my 10th birthday. I got Cousteau to sign it at a dive show a few years later. It's worth a few bucks because of his signature."

"Aren't you afraid it will be stolen?"

"We lock it in the safe when we're not here. What can I do you for? I can't imagine I have something the SeaSide Inn doesn't. Other than a first edition of *The Silent World*, signed by the author, that is."

Danny had been looking at the rental equipment. Now he said, "We need a tank O-ring. We're hoping we won't have to go all the way back to the inn to get one."

Les opened a drawer under the counter and pulled out a small bag. He took several black O-rings out of the bag and handed them to Danny. "Here you go."

"Thanks," Danny said. "How much do I owe you?"

"On the house," Les said. "I heard Ryan and Sara are out of jail. Does that mean the cops have cleared them?"

"We don't know," I said. "Westwood is being close-mouthed. We don't think they're guilty. Do you?"

Les walked to a corner and picked up a well-used wooden baseball bat. At first I thought he was going to take a swing at me. Instead, he squashed a cockroach that had ventured out from under the counter.

A whiteboard on the wall had today's date along with "Les" and "Paul" printed on it and, under each name, a series of hash marks. Les added a mark under "Les" — I counted nine. There were five marks under "Paul."

Les stuck the bat in a trash basket, rubbed the roach off the end and returned the bat to its corner. "Paul and I have a contest. The one who kills the most roaches or one scorpion gets Sunday off."

"There are scorpions on the island?" I asked.

"Oh yes. The little buggers like to hide in wetsuits. I shake mine out before I put it on, but I've been stung several times. Roaches and scorpions are crustaceans you know, cousins of lobsters. Their hard shells make them hard to kill."

The topic made me nauseous. I repeated my question. "Do you think the Millers are guilty?"

Les blinked. "Of course not."

"Someone told us you didn't much like Van Slyke," I said.

Les nodded. "He sold my shop," he said. "I could've gotten the money but he refused to give me enough time."

"And Paul is the new owner?" I asked.

"No. His dad, Bram Metsalaer, is the owner. Paul's the manager. Not that he has any real interest in the job. It cuts into his party time."

"Why did his dad buy the shop?" I asked.

"It was cheap and he hoped it would keep Paul out of trouble. He owns the resort, too, bought it about five years ago. He keeps saying he's going to renovate it and the dive shop but I don't think he's got the funds."

"Weasel must be fried by now, Cinnamon," Danny said. "We should go."

We said our goodbyes. Les fired up the compressor and attached a fill hose to another tank.

Chapter 20

Back at Something Special, we were flabbergasted to find our gear shaded by a large blue umbrella and Weasel nowhere in sight.

"I'll be right there," a voice yelled. We looked up to see Weasel standing on the middle deck of the *California Girl* with several other people.

He disappeared from view, reappearing on the main deck. He walked down the gangplank and made the small leap from the concrete wall to the sand, then turned to wave at the people he'd just left.

"Thanks a lot," he called. "See you tonight."

"You know the owners of that boat?" I asked.

"I didn't when you left but I do now," Weasel grinned. "They saw me sitting in the sun and took pity on me. They sent a deckhand over with the umbrella and invited me to come aboard for a cold drink. Turns out the owner is a diver. He wants to meet you. We're all invited to dinner on the boat tonight. Wait till you see the *California Girl*. She's a beauty."

He described the boat enthusiastically as we got ready for the dive.

Something Special lived up to its name. We swam the short distance across the sand to a steeply sloping drop-off, which covered with low profile coral heads. On our meandering way to the bottom at 80 feet, we came across two frogfish, one about four inches long, the other no more than three. Frogfish usually change colors to match their surroundings but these were bright yellow and stood out like beacons on the green corals. A school of tiny fry swarmed around the first one. We watched the frogfish extend a fleshy appendage from the top of its head that functioned as a fishing lure. When fry tried to eat the lure, the frogfish opened its oversized mouth and engulfed them. Danny got great video of the action and I got some excellent stills.

After that we were paparazzi to a sharptail snake eel. About two feet long, the pale green creature had large, light yellow spots. It ignored us and went about its business, poking its head into crevices, crannies and holes, looking for tasty morsels. We saw a couple of spotted morays peering out from under small coral heads and several greenish-brown moray eels hidden among the huge boulders that formed the breakwater. We could only see parts of these giants: a large head with big black eyes and a snub nose, a mouth filled with needle sharp teeth, and a paddle-like tail.

We spent a lot of time in the shallows near the breakwater, looking for frogfish among the small pink sponges and photographing little creatures hiding in rubber tires and small coral heads. The most intriguing find was a minute juvenile pufferfish, black with small white dots. At first, I thought it was a piece of debris.

We surfaced exhilarated. This had been our very best Bonamer dive.

While we were removing our fins in shallow water Weasel said, "That does it, I'm taking up underwater videography. You got great footage of that frogfish, didn't you, Danny?"

"I don't like to brag," Danny began, "but..."

"You do like to brag," I interrupted, "and your video is probably terrific."

"You're right, as usual," Danny said, throwing modesty to the wind. "The store where I rented my system is on the way home. Want to stop there, Weasel?"

"Yes, he does," I said. "Otherwise he'll be mooching your stuff."

The store didn't have another rental unit like Danny's but it did have a top of the line video system for sale, It wasn't cheap.

"What do you think?" Weasel asked. "I don't think I'll outgrow it anytime soon and I already know what it does because I've sold a couple at Greene's."

"Dad will give you a better price, though," I pointed out.

"I need it now," Weasel said. He produced a platinum charge card and bought the entire system. Danny and I were astounded.

Later, on the way back to the inn, Weasel answered our

---

unspoken question. "Since my parents wanted me to get an education, the trust is fairly generous as long as I'm in school."

"No wonder you've put off graduating," I teased.

Back at the SeaSide Inn, we unloaded the van, rinsed the sand off our gear and put it in our lockers to drip dry. In our apartment, Danny and I worked on our camera systems and helped Weasel ready his for its initial dive.

Because we didn't want to rush through lunch and camera preparation, we decided not to go out on a boat and make our dive off the SeaSide Inn pier instead.

Weasel has always seemed to cruise through life on autopilot, so his excitement about his new toys was fun to see. In a complete turnaround, he was in the water first and waited impatiently for us to join him.

Since we'd gone south on our last pier dive, Danny decided we'd go north on this one. Weasel and I were happy to let him lead.

Bonamer was hit by storm surge from a wrong way hurricane several years ago. The SeaSide Inn's pier had been pulled out of the water before that happened. Right next door, however, the GrapeTree Resort's three permanent piers had suffered extensive damage, as had the guest rooms and the two restaurants on the shoreline. Near the edge of the drop-off, we found furnishings that had been swept out to sea, including a bent and rusty patio chair and table. We took turns sitting in the chair and mugging for the camera.

Danny led us down the drop-off to a sandy plain at 70 feet. As before, a small school of tarpon hovered at the edge of visibility. Weasel started toward them. Danny knew the fish would continue to move out to sea, so he went after Weasel and brought him back.

That's when we saw the big barracuda. These fish act stealthy and look menacing. They have sharp, pointed teeth, visible when they open and close their mouths. About five feet long, this one appeared to be following us. Weasel glanced at it and moved closer to Danny. I decided to show him just how harmless the fish was. Slowly but steadily, I swam toward it. The fish held its ground until I was within 10 feet, then turned and fled.

We came across several large schools of grunts among the coral heads that lined the drop-off. They hung nearly motionless a few feet above the bottom and paid little attention to us, which made it easy to get photos.

Danny signaled it was time to turn around. We made our way up the slope to shallower water and headed back to the SeaSide Inn.

As we climbed up the ladder on the end of the pier Weasel said, "That was very nice but can we go back to Something Special tomorrow? I have to video a frogfish."

"Maybe we could get Laurie to take us there on the morning boat," I suggested.

We rinsed our gear, hung it in our lockers and went upstairs. Weasel took his camera out of its housing and plugged it into the TV so Danny and I could view and critique his footage.

I only had one suggestion. "You can get a lot closer to a barracuda," I pointed out. "They won't hurt you."

"Ha!" Weasel said.

"It's true," Danny said. "There were a bunch of barracuda attacks in Florida several years ago but they all involved fishermen. The barracuda were hooked and pulled into boats or jumped into them accidentally, biting the guys who caught them. In one case, a barracuda flopped into the galley of a houseboat and bit the fisherman's wife, who was fixing lunch. These fish don't attack divers."

"Right," Weasel was not convinced.

We heard the boats come in and waited until the passengers dispersed before going downstairs. Danny told Ryan and Sara about our dinner invitation and asked to borrow the van. In the dive shop, we asked Laurie if she would take us to Something Special in the morning and she readily agreed.

Weasel remained in the dive shop when Danny and I went outside to sign-up for spots on Laurie's boat the next day. Rejoining us in our apartment, he settled into his regular spot on the sofa, then said: "The owner of the *California Girl* is a former CEO of a large oil company headquartered in Chicago. He's retired now and lives in San Diego. He and his wife spend a lot of time on the boat, diving and cruising. They've been all over the world. If there's a long ocean voyage involved, they send the boat ahead, then fly over in their private jet to meet it. Friends and family hook up with them from time to time. They're fun people. I think you'll like them."

For Weasel, not noted for being forthcoming about anything, this was a speech of near epic proportions.

Chapter 21

Fifteen minutes before the appointed time, we piled into the van and drove north. It was dusk and the *California Girl* was lit up like a Christmas tree, making her even more impressive than she'd been during the day.

A crewmember in an immaculate white uniform with gold trim met us as we stepped aboard and led the way to the boat's huge saloon, aglow with polished brass fixtures, gleaming teak and plush light blue carpeting. There was a bar at one end and, near the center, a large round table, resplendent with white linens, china and crystal.

Our host and his wife were seated on a blue velvet sofa. A matching sofa and chairs were grouped around a beautiful glass-topped cocktail table, its base a bronze sculpture of three dolphins.

Our host rose and strode toward us with his hand extended and an infectious grin on his face. His gray-green eyes were bright behind rimless glasses. "Hi, I'm Todd and this is my wife, Caroline."

Deeply tanned, Todd Graham was nearly six feet tall, with a full head of immaculately groomed silver hair.

Caroline was a slender blonde attired in spotless white linen slacks and a sleeveless red top. Gold bracelets dangled from her arms and diamond earrings glittered in her ears. Like her husband, she was in wonderful shape for her age but her face looked 20 years younger than the rest of her. Ah, the joys of great wealth and plastic surgery.

Danny shook hands with our host. "Good to see you again, Todd. I didn't know you owned the *California Girl*."

Todd said, "Welcome aboard."

I was confused. "You know each other?"

"Todd and Caroline were on my boat yesterday," Danny said. They are the ones who told me about Something Special."

"I thought you had to be a SeaSide Inn guest to go out on their boats," Weasel said.

"Ryan takes walk-ons if he has space. My boat wasn't full, so the Grahams got to dive with us. Besides, they're long-time SeaSide Inn customers."

"We've dived with Laurie, Sara and Ryan on previous trips," Todd said. "We can't believe the police suspect the Millers of murdering anyone. Weasel told us they were out of jail. How are they doing?"

"As well as could be expected," Danny said. "None of us have any idea why the cops picked them up."

"The laws on Bonamer are different than those in the States," I said. "You have to have evidence of wrong-doing to put people in jail there."

A uniformed crewmember asked for drink orders and began to fill them. Todd gestured toward the blue sofas and invited us to sit.

When we were settled he said: "Discussions of unpleasant subjects are hereby banned for the rest of the evening. Caroline and I invited you to dinner so we could talk about diving. It's our favorite activity and we do it every chance we get. We're going to Australia this winter and are thinking about visiting Fiji next year. We've got to fit the Caymans and Bahamas into our schedule again soon, too."

"What a dream life," I said. "Do you hire a dive guide in each place you visit?"

"Sometimes," Todd said. "But we usually have an instructor on our boat crew. His job is to maintain our gear, research the best places to dive and be our buddy. We have a couple of compressors and a dinghy to take us to sites."

I'd seen the "dinghy" tied to the *California Girl*'s stern. It was a cabin cruiser about 25 feet long.

After our drinks were served. Todd asked, "Would you like a tour of our boat?"

"We'd love it," Danny answered.

Even though Weasel had described the yacht in detail I was overwhelmed by it. The owners' stateroom was enormous and beautifully decorated. It had his and her bathrooms. The engine room gleamed (dive store owner Danny salivated over the twin air compressors) and the galley was a chef's dream. Even the crew cabins were spacious and well appointed.

"On a boat this size, the crew's comfort is essential," Todd explained. "If they're not happy we won't be."

As he opened the door of one cabin he said: "This is our dive instructor's suite, currently empty. Our last instructor, Kyle, went bike riding in the national park the day we arrived and fractured his arm. It was a very bad break and we had to send him home."

The instructor's suite had a queen-sized bed, desk/chair and a sofa, along with a large, flat screen TV. The dominant color was blue; the bedspread, curtains and towels had a marine life motif. I could see myself living in that room.

Our last stop was the dive locker on the main deck, which contained eight complete sets of scuba gear, all of them new and state of the art. There was even a selection of neoprene suits in different sizes.

"Our guests don't have to bring any equipment with them," Todd said proudly. "And if they're not yet divers, our instructor can certify them while they're on the boat."

We returned to the saloon, dazzled. The evening passed in a haze. We met several more crewmembers and were served a wonderful dinner. There was a lot of laughter.

Afterward we moved to the fan deck, where we sipped after-dinner drinks and enjoyed the warm night air. The ocean was absolutely calm.

"If you ever need a dive buddy, I'm available," Weasel said.

"I'm an even better buddy," Danny said. "Plus I'm an instructor and have my captain's license."

Todd laughed. "Actually, we invited you here tonight because we wanted to talk to you about that. As I said earlier, we lost our instructor recently. That's why we ended up on a SeaSide Inn boat. We're leaving soon and need to hire a replacement.

"We've checked out several local instructors but the person we were most impressed with was you, Danny. You have all the skills we need plus a great personality. We'd love having you work for us. Think about it — you'd get paid for diving and cruising the world. The salary's negotiable. Tell us what you want. We can probably accommodate you."

Danny's eyebrows went sky-high. He wasn't expecting a job offer of any kind, let alone one like that. Weasel and I shot him envious looks. His reply, however, was a surprise.

"I'll have to think about it. I've got a business to run in California and a nine year old son who'd miss me if I was gone for very long." He looked at me and added, "Besides, Cinnamon would hate it if I dived the world without her."

Todd chuckled. "Weasel told us what a terrific photographer you are, Cinnamon. We're prepared to offer you a job as *California Girl*'s first underwater photo pro. We'd love to have someone documenting our and our guests' adventures."

Todd looked at Weasel. "We love having dive buddies. We'd expect to see you several times a year.

"Try it for six months, Danny. If you don't like it, I'll send you home on my jet."

Weasel and I could hardly contain our joy. Danny said, "I'll sleep on it and let you know tomorrow."

Back in the van later, Weasel and I exploded.

"You are one cool negotiator," Weasel said. "Anyone else would have said yes right away. What are you holding out for?"

"Wow," I said. "Getting paid for diving the world and taking pictures. Fantastic!"

Danny frowned. "I'm not trying to leverage a bigger salary or any other perk; I'm trying to let the Grahams down gently. I don't want the job."

"What?" Weasel and I shouted in unison. "Are you nuts?"

"Those people are strangers. We don't really know anything about them. They were on their best behavior tonight. And while the *California Girl* is a big boat, she's a pretty small place to spend all day, every day, for six months."

"But Danny, diving the world and getting paid for it? Couldn't you just try it for six months? After all, I'd be with you," I pleaded.

"I don't want the job."

I hoped for but didn't hear any doubt in his voice.

When we got back to the SeaSide Inn, the lights were still on in the Miller's house. Weasel and I dragged Danny to their front door. Often talking at the same time, we blurted out the details of Danny's job offer. Sara and Ryan were as incredulous as we were that he planned to turn it down.

"I can't believe you're not going to take it," Sara said. "That's a once in a lifetime opportunity."

Danny dug in his heels. "My business wouldn't survive six months without me. Besides, Sam looks forward to spending the summers with me. I can't disappoint him."

"Take Sam with you," Sara urged. "I'd bet the Grahams would love to have him on board. How many kids get to cruise the oceans on a luxury yacht? It would be something he'd never forget."

"It would be fun for a couple of weeks," Danny agreed. "Not the whole summer. He'd be bored being the only kid on the boat. If he was older and could dive, I might consider it. Not now, however. He's too young. Besides, his mother would never agree to it."

That's when I realized there was absolutely no chance Danny would change his mind. His son lived with his mother, Danny's ex-wife, in San Francisco. The weeks Sam spent in Cliffview each summer were the high points of his and his dad's year. Sam played summer league baseball; Danny was the team's coach. They attended Dodgers games in LA and went boogie boarding off Cliffview's beach. Sam and a friend often went out on the dive boats with Danny, Weasel and me. They fished, snorkeled and had a great time.

I stole a glance at Weasel, whose face mirrored my disappointment. I recognized the speculation in his eyes. Like me, he was wondering how quickly he could get his instructor's certification so he'd be eligible for the *California Girl* job.

I went to bed hoping against hope that Danny would have some revelation that would change his mind. He didn't. The next morning he called Todd from the dive shop and told him he wouldn't be joining the crew of the *California Girl*. Ryan and Laurie heard him on the phone. While they didn't say so, it was pretty obvious they thought he was making a big mistake.

Danny's decision, however, was temporarily forgotten when the latest issue of the Bonamer Current was delivered to the dive store. The headline on the little island newspaper read: "Police Say Developer Died of Natural Causes."

Chapter 22

According to the newspaper, the police had known how Van Slyke died since the autopsy but hadn't released that information because they still had questions about the circumstances.

"Van Slyke didn't die underwater, he had a fatal heart attack on land," Westwood was quoted as saying. "Afterward, his body was dumped in the harbor. Later still, it was tied to two tires under the pier. We would like whoever did this to explain their actions."

While I was speechless, Ryan was furious. "We spent 24 hours in jail for no reason. I'm calling my lawyer."

I don't remember much about the rest of that day. The revelation that Van Slyke hadn't been murdered and the police had known that almost from the beginning was a stunner. Now I understood why they hadn't conducted what I considered a proper investigation.

I was also extremely disappointed that Danny had turned down the *California Girl* job. That made me crabby. Maybe he didn't want to dive exotic locales but I sure did, especially for free.

A dark cloud hovered over Weasel's head as well. Both of us sulked. While Danny must have noticed our bad behavior, he didn't comment on it.

We made two dives that day. Although they were fun, they were only temporary distractions.

Later, Weasel, Danny and I hunkered down around the kitchen table and fiddled gloomily with our camera systems. We were discussing what to have for dinner when Ryan knocked on the door and entered, his face creased with worry.

"Sara's missing," he said, his voice strained. "I've called the police."

"Since when?" I asked.

"Today was her day off. She was supposed to have lunch with Karin at a new restaurant in Lac Bay. I expected her back this afternoon."

"She's only a few hours late," I pointed out.

"I called Karin," Ryan went on. "They didn't go to Lac Bay. They had lunch at the Green Iguana. Sara left there about 1:00. She didn't say where she was going. I can't imagine where she could be. I've got to go back to the house, the police should be here any minute."

"I'll come with you," Danny said.

"Me, too," I said.

Weasel joined us as we trooped over to the Miller home.

Ryan paced back and forth in his living room. It was obvious he had a lot on his mind but he couldn't or wouldn't talk about it. I wondered if Sara was already off the island.

Westwood arrived about 30 minutes later. By then Ryan was so tightly wound he was ready to explode. He told Westwood what he had told us, adding one rather important detail.

"Sara has received several anonymous e-mails in the past few weeks that claimed Laurie and I were having an affair. She didn't tell me about them; I found them in her e-mail inbox tonight. I've printed out copies for you." He handed Westwood a sheaf of papers.

"Any idea who sent them?" Westwood asked.

"No. And before you ask, the e-mails aren't true. Laurie and I had a one night stand last year, one Sara and everybody on the island knows about. There was nothing before that and there's been absolutely nothing since."

"Did your wife take anything with her when she left today?" Westwood asked.

Ryan looked surprised. "I don't know," he said. "I was out on a boat." He dashed into the bedroom. When he returned he said: "Her airplane carryon and purse are gone. I don't know if anything else is missing. She has a lot of clothes. She could have taken some of them and I wouldn't know."

"What about money?" Westwood asked.

Ryan disappeared into the bedroom again. When he came back, he looked ill. "There was emergency money in our safe. Most of it is gone. So is Sara's passport."

"I'd check my bank account if I were you," Westwood advised.

"Do you have a photo of Sara?"

Ryan went back into the bedroom and brought out a small color photo of Sara and him, which he handed to Westwood. "Can you find out if she left the island by air?"

"Already checked," Westwood said. "She didn't fly out today and she doesn't have reservations on any flight in the future, at least not under her own name."

"Her car's gone," Ryan said.

"My officers are already looking for it," Westwood said. "Who are Sara's closest friends?"

"Karin Van Slyke is the only person on the island that she spends any time with," Ryan said.

"Guess I better have a little chat with her. Here's my cell phone number. Call me right away if you hear from her."

The SeaSide Inn had a built-in barbecue grill at the foot of the pier, in front of a gazebo. Ryan and Laurie held scuba classes there and guests prepared meals and enjoyed cocktails at sunset there as well.

While Danny thinks he's good at barbecuing, few people like their food as well done (i.e., resembling charcoal briquettes) as he does. To keep him away from the grill, I sent him to the store to buy coleslaw ingredients and asked Weasel to cook the chicken as soon as he was out of the door.

We invited Ryan to join us but he declined. He was going to call Sara's family and friends in the States to ask if they knew where she was. I thought he was over-reacting. She hadn't even been gone 12 hours.

In our apartment I made coleslaw while Danny cooked three potatoes in the microwave oven. We took the food and a pitcher of iced tea to the gazebo and watched the sun set beyond Little Bonamer as the chicken grilled. Weasel hovered over the chicken, shooing Danny away, and the fowl ended up cooked perfectly.

Halfway through the meal I suddenly remembered something. "What happened to your divemaster class?" I asked.

Weasel studied his plate. "Laurie said there wasn't enough time to complete it before I went home. She said she'll refund the money the next time she gets paid."

"You can finish the class with me in Cliffview," Danny offered, "no charge."

"Great!"

Danny looked at me. "You can take the class with him, Cinnamon. You have to be a divemaster before you can become an instructor and work on the *California Girl*."

I blushed. The man was a mind reader. "I just might do that."

I changed the subject. "Any idea where Sara might be?"

"No," Danny answered.

"Do you think she left the island?" Weasel asked.

"Possibly. She wasn't happy here," I said. "She missed her family and didn't like working in the dive shop. She's claustrophobic and hates being in small places. Oh, did you know she's a vegan?"

"No wonder she's so skinny," Weasel said. "Fresh vegetables are hard to come by here."

Chapter 23

Laurie didn't look forward to Sara's days off because she had to spend those afternoons in the SeaSide Inn's dive shop instead of out on a boat. Besides, Sara's being gone didn't mean she got to spend any time alone with Ryan. When he was in the shop, she was out on a boat. And when she was in the shop, he was out on a boat. The rare times they were in the same place, they were busy helping customers or performing some other task separately.

Laurie wondered how Sara could spend five days a week in the store. Laurie couldn't have done it. Not even to be near Ryan. What Laurie loved about her job was running the boat and diving. She knew Sara wanted to go out on the boats more often and Ryan had agreed that that would happen — some day.

If Sara knew why he put her off she would be even more unhappy than she already was. Laurie wanted Sara to find out but didn't know how to leak knowledge only she and Ryan were privy to without alienating him.

The only thing that made being in the shop bearable for Laurie was writing her column for the SeaSide Inn's website. There were few to no customers until Ryan's boat returned so there was plenty of time to work on it. Today, she went into Ryan's office and jumped on the internet, accessing one of her private e-mail accounts. At home at the end of each day she made notations about what she'd seen on her dives and stored the document as an e-mail draft. Today, all she had to do was pull up the draft, edit it and post it on the website.

Laurie enjoyed writing the column, which described the critters she saw and what they were doing. She did a lot of research on the internet and loved being able to slip in small bits of information that weren't commonly known. The website got lots of hits because of the column and quite a few of those who read it became SeaSide Inn customers.

Today Laurie wrote:

"The brown seahorse at Petrie's Pillar is definitely pregnant, which means it's a male. His little round tummy is so cute! I'll let you know when the babies are born.

"The yellow frogfish at Hands Off has moved from a group of yellow sponges to a deeper sponge of a different color. It may have moved because it got tired of visitors so I'm taking it off the tour for a while. If you find it, please give it some privacy.

"The male sergeant majors are sprucing up their nests in hopes of attracting females to lay their eggs. Look for patches of pink algae on the sides of rocks and pier pilings. The males are aggressive about protecting their nests, so don't get too close or you might get your ear nipped.

"Wednesday, at the dive site off Little Bonamer known as Capt. Don's, I found a small octopus right under the boat. Its den is a hole in the sand. If you stay very still the octo might come all the way out to look at you — it did for us!"

Laurie revised, edited and added to her draft until it was finally ready to post. Once that was done, she answered e-mails from guests. Some just wanted to chat, some sent photos of creatures they hoped she could identify, some just wanted to make sure she would be around on their next visit so they could dive with her.

The inn only had one computer, which Laurie, Sara and Ryan used. They each had a SeaSide e-mail account that all of them could access. They all also had private, web-based accounts. Laurie had found Ryan's and figured out his password, "Seaside," on the first try. She had eventually gotten into Sara's account as well.

Ryan's messages were pretty boring. He only had a few regular correspondents, mostly family members in the States. Sometimes one of them included Ryan's original message when replying. From those Laurie discovered that Ryan was less than truthful. According to him, life on Bonamer was hunky-dory and he, Sara and the inn were doing great.

Yeah right, Laurie thought. You had to borrow money from me to keep the inn from closing and Sara hates living on Bonamer. The two of you are suspects in the murder of a "prominent citizen" and just spent the night in the Bonamer jail. Life, indeed, was wonderful.

Sara's e-mails were also uninteresting. Her sister and mother wrote nearly every day and she got frequent messages from a female friend in Oregon. The e-mails usually included Sara's original messages, which were almost always rants about the inconveniences of life on Bonamer. When Laurie first started reading them, the messages Sara received from her correspondents expressed sympathy that she had to endure such hardships. Now they rarely referred to them. Laurie figured the sister, mother and friend had grown as tired as she had about hearing Sara complain over and over about the same things.

Laurie scrolled quickly through Sara's messages. About a month ago she had come across an e-mail from someone using the alias, "Tattletale." Several more had arrived since then. All of them claimed that Laurie and Ryan were having an affair. They were crudely written and Laurie thought she knew who was sending them though she didn't know why. She wanted the e-mails to continue, hoping they would make Sara so miserable she would leave the island and return to the States, where life was so much better than it was here.

There was no new message from Tattletale. Laurie signed out of Sara's e-mail and doodled around on the internet until she heard Ryan's boat return. After that, the two of them were busy for nearly an hour, helping the five or six people who wanted to buy T-shirts, tank tops and dive accessories and ask questions about nearly everything. When only a couple of customers remained, Laurie went to the compressor room and started filling tanks. She had finished and was in the shop collecting her stuff prior to heading home when Ryan appeared.

"Have you seen Sara today?"

Laurie shook her head.

"Well she's not home yet. She should be back by now. She was only supposed to have lunch with Karin."

Ryan went into his office and picked up the phone. He didn't close the door.

"Hey Karin. Do you know where Sara is?"

Ryan listened for a bit, then said, "So you didn't go to Lac Bay?"

After another brief silence he said, "Okay. Thanks a lot. If you do see or hear from her, please tell her to call me. She's not answering her cell phone and I'm getting worried."

Ryan hung up the phone and came out of his office, his brow furrowed.

"Sara and Karin had lunch at the Green Iguana. Sara left there about 1:00. Karin thought she was going home. I just can't imagine where she could be and why she hasn't called me."

Before Laurie could comment, Ryan turned, left the shop and headed for his house. Laurie locked everything up and got in her car. On the way home she stopped at a drugstore. The town was full of people and she had to park in the lot across from the police station. As she was getting ready to leave, she saw a police car head down the road that passed the SeaSide Inn. Maybe Ryan had reported Sara missing.

Laurie could hardly contain her joy. Had Sara really left Bonamer? She got in her car and followed the cruiser to the inn, watching as Officer Westwood parked in the tiny lot and disappeared through the gate that led to Ryan's house.

About half an hour later, Westwood came out and drove away.

Laurie sat in her car for a few minutes, struggling with her emotions. Then she went to Ryan's house. He answered her knock right away but the light in his eyes died when he saw her. Laurie felt the first pangs of misgiving.

"Have you found Sara?" he asked.

"No. Can I come in?"

Ryan led her to the living room. He seemed distracted, or maybe distraught, Laurie couldn't tell which.

"She took her passport and some money," Ryan said. "Why would she do that? Where would she go? Do you have any ideas?"

Laurie summoned her courage. It was now or never. "Sara wasn't happy living on Bonamer. You had to know that. Everybody knows that. She's probably gone back to the States. But it's not a bad thing she left."

Ryan frowned. "What?"

"You don't need her and her constant whining. You and I can run the inn fine without her. We'd only need to hire one other person."

Laurie took a deep breath and went on. "I know how you feel about me, Ryan. I feel the same way about you."

The look on Ryan's face made Laurie's heart sink. It was not what she'd expected.

Ryan spoke slowly and carefully. "You're my right hand,

Laurie. I don't know what I'd do without you. But I love Sara. I love my wife. If I've misled you somehow I'm sorry, Babe."

Laurie died a thousand deaths. Her face flushed bright red. The pity she saw on Ryan's face was unbearable.

"I thought…" she began. But then she realized she hadn't thought at all, she'd only hoped. Laurie was frozen in place for a few minutes. Time stood still. Finally, she turned and walked away.

Somehow she got back to her car and climbed inside, feeling stunned and sick to her stomach. Now what? She couldn't go back to the SeaSide Inn, not ever. It would be too humiliating.

Laurie started the car and headed home. On the way, she passed the *California Girl*. Todd Graham had offered her the instructor job two years ago and again this year, before he tried to hire Danny. She had turned him down both times without telling anyone because she didn't want to cause trouble between the Grahams and the Millers and most especially, she couldn't leave Ryan.

Laurie pulled off to the side of the road and took her cell phone out of her purse. She found Graham's phone number and dialed it.

"Todd? This is Laurie Cook. Are you still looking for an instructor?"

Chapter 24

Our night dive off the SeaSide Inn Pier was a disaster. My strobe let me take four photos, then died. All three of us ascended and milled around on the surface while I checked it out. There didn't seem to be any water inside so it hadn't flooded, yet it refused to work.

My camera system is bulky and I didn't want to carry it around if I couldn't use it. I swam back to the pier, where I planned to stash the camera in one of the boats.

Once out of the water, I didn't want to go back in. Without my camera, I'd feel naked. If we found something unusual I'd be upset because I couldn't photograph it. I wanted to return to our apartment and work on the strobe.

Danny and Weasel, however, were floating on the surface quite a distance away. I'd have to shout my intentions to them and there was no guarantee they'd understand what I said.

I had no choice. I stowed the camera in Ryan's boat, covered it with a towel and swam out to join the guys.

Danny always carried three lights so he loaned me one of his and we descended, with Weasel leading the way and giving me a front seat view of what happened next.

To compensate for the buoyancy of his new camera system, Weasel had added weight to his weightbelt, a little too much it appeared. He was fiddling with the controls of his housing when he hit the bottom with a thud. He reacted by using a bare hand (gloves are forbidden on Bonamer) to steady himself and touched a small stand of fire coral. The yelp he uttered drew Danny's attention and we both trained our lights on him.

Fire coral stings. I'd stumbled into it years ago on my first Caribbean trip. For a few minutes the pain was so intense it brought tears of agony. Within hours, an ugly, itchy rash broke out where skin and coral had made contact. When that went away the skin peeled off. It was a couple of months before my arm looked normal.

We knelt on the sand and had a powwow conducted with light movement, head shaking and hand signals. I wanted to abort the dive, Danny didn't. Weasel examined his hand. When he figured out he wasn't going to die, he sided with Danny.

We resumed the dive. I found an octopus out hunting for dinner. Trying to frighten us into leaving it alone, it sprouted fleshy horns and flashed colors ranging from brown to bright red. As Danny and Weasel filmed it, one of Danny's video lights died. We returned to the surface and milled around some more. The light hadn't flooded and Danny still had one that worked so we descended once again.

We were headed down the drop-off when the light I'd borrowed from Danny ran out of power. Before I could swim over to him, I began having trouble breathing. When I checked my air supply I was shocked to find my tank was virtually empty. Neither Danny nor Weasel was nearby, so I slowly headed to the surface, sucking on my regulator as I rose and getting a little air as the water pressure decreased and the air coming out of the tank expanded.

I reached the surface safely and floated there, waiting for Danny and Weasel to notice I was gone. It was annoying how long that took. Their lights had been poking casually this way and that in the dark; when they began to swing around wildly, I knew they had finally missed me. Neither thought to look up. As good buddies should, however, they ascended after a few minutes.

Each of us had placed a different color light on our tank valve for this dive. Danny recognized my blue one as he broke the surface. "Cinnamon," he gasped, spitting out his regulator. "Are you okay? What happened?"

"I ran out of air," I said. "The tank must not have been full. I don't remember checking it before the dive."

"That's it," Danny said. "This freakin' dive is over. We're going in."

It wasn't quite that easy. Strong currents are rare off Bonamer but now we realized we had been in one for quite a while. We'd spent much more time on the surface than usual and had been so busy solving problems we hadn't noticed how fast we'd been moving.

We had to swim against the current to get back to the SeaSide's pier. Luckily, the gazebo has a distinctive green light on it so it was easy to find in the dark. Luckily also, we're all in pretty good shape, though I'm glad I didn't have to drag a camera system with me.

When we finally climbed up the ladder to the pier Danny said, "How could you not check your tank pressure before diving?"

"How could you not notice the current had picked up?" I retorted.

"What the did I put my hand on?" Weasel asked. "Man, did that sting. It still hurts."

Ryan heard the commotion and came out to investigate. When we told him what had happened he said, "Laurie filled the tanks this afternoon. I'll have to talk to her about that tomorrow."

"Any word on Sara?" Danny asked.

"They found her car in the North Shore Resort parking lot," Ryan said. "I have no idea what that means."

He ran his fingers through his hair. "I don't know if she's coming back. I guess I'd better hire another instructor. Until I do, can you run one of the boats, Danny? I'll mind the store tomorrow."

Of course Danny agreed. After we rinsed and stowed our gear, Weasel and I wrote our numbers on the sign-up board for the morning dive on his boat.

After we showered, I tried a new synch cord on my strobe and was relieved when it worked. Danny's video light, however, could not be revived.

"Maybe you can rent one of those, too," I said.

Weasel was lucky. The skin where he'd touched the fire coral was red but there was no rash.

Exhausted, we all went to bed.

Chapter 25

I slept like a dead woman. I don't remember dreaming. I didn't even get up in the middle of the night to pee. And the compressor didn't wake me; Danny did.

It was eerily quiet for 8:00 am at the SeaSide Inn.

"Something's wrong, Sunshine," Danny said. "The dive shop is locked. Ryan and the van are gone."

"I don't know where Laurie is. I called her from the GrapeTree Resort office. She didn't answer her cell.

"We also got these back," Danny held my stolen laptop in one hand, his video camera in the other. "They were on our doorstep this morning. They aren't damaged."

"Let's go see Westwood," I said. "Maybe he knows what's going on."

We awakened Weasel before we left. He said, "I'll stay here in case Ryan or Laurie shows up."

It was already hot and I was dripping with perspiration by the time we got to the police station. Our trip was in vain. Westwood wasn't there and the man at the desk refused to tell us anything. He wouldn't let us report Ryan and Laurie missing either, though he noted the return of our stolen equipment before we headed back to the inn.

I said, "What kind of thief returns what he's stolen?"

"Don't know, don't care," Danny said. "I'm just glad to have my camera back and in good shape."

"What are we going to do today?" I asked.

"Let's stop by the GrapeTree," Danny suggested. "Maybe we and the rest of the SeaSide's guests can dive with them."

The GrapeTree was just north of the SeaSide Inn and we passed it every time we went to or from town. An old but recently renovated resort, it had three piers and five boats. The dive shop was at the base of its southernmost pier and right next door to Ryan and Sara's house. From the SeaSide's pier and gazebo, we had often watched GrapeTree guests board their dive boats and head out to sea.

We followed the signs to the dive shop. Danny said: "We're guests at the SeaSide Inn and they've cancelled the diving today. Any chance we can dive with you?"

The man behind the counter looked at the clock. "Just you or all the inn's guests?"

"Can you take all of us?"

"If you have at least eight people, I can schedule a boat to take you out at two o'clock," the man said. "You can also rent tanks from us and dive off our pier anytime."

Danny looked at me. "Pier okay?" he asked.

"Fine," I said.

"Put us down for the pier," Danny said. "We'll talk to the rest of the guests and suggest they come see you if they want to dive today."

Nothing had changed at the SeaSide Inn. Neither Ryan nor Laurie had shown up. Several unhappy guests were sitting on the pool deck, grumbling about the lack of diving. We explained the GrapeTree's offer and left them to discuss it. Then Danny and I split up and started knocking on guestroom doors. When we'd talked to everyone, we went upstairs to tell Weasel what was going on. He was reviewing video he'd shot on our night dive.

"I could do a pier dive," he said.

I had been thinking. "You guys go," I said. "I want to walk down to the Green Iguana and talk to Karin. She was the last person to see Sara."

The Green Iguana was a 10-minute walk south of the SeaSide Inn and the site of the No Tees meeting we'd attended. It was the largest resort on the island and its two-story buildings were scattered across several nicely landscaped acres. Karin's boutique was in the main building, which housed the registration desk, three restaurants, a casino and several small shops.

The boutique carried high-end resort clothing and accessories, including everything from cocktail dresses and swimsuit cover-ups to designer sunglasses and costume jewelry. Karin was sorting through a rack of sundresses when I came in.

"Has Sara turned up?"

"No," I said. "Have you heard from her?"

Karin shook her head.

"Do you know where she might be?"

"No."

"You seemed to have been the last person who saw her," I said. "Did she seem upset?"

"Wouldn't you be if you'd just spent the night in jail?"

"Did she mention leaving the island?

"No."

"Was she unhappy about anything else?"

Karin made a dismissive gesture with her hand. "Sara is always unhappy. She complains constantly about a lot of little things that don't matter. I stopped listening a long time ago."

I asked a few more questions and received more unenlightening answers. Frustrated, I left the boutique. I had learned absolutely nothing new.

The SeaSide Inn was quiet. The dive store was still closed and there was no sign of Ryan or Laurie. I didn't see any guests and assumed they were all over at the GrapeTree.

I decided to walk downtown and check in with the police. Maybe Westwood was there and would talk to me.

I was surprised to find the SeaSide Inn's van in the police station parking lot. I was even more surprised when the front door opened and Ryan came out. His face was gray with fatigue and lined with worry. He looked unkempt. His T-shirt was rumpled and dirty and he needed a shave.

"What's going on? Where's Laurie? Any word on Sara?"

"Let's get out of here," Ryan said.

We climbed into the van. Instead of heading toward the SeaSide Inn, Ryan drove north on the road that ran through the middle of the island.

"I'm so hungry I'm dizzy. I've got to eat something," he explained. "And I don't want to run into anyone I know."

A five-minute drive took us to an area where the road was lined with several small, one-story buildings: an appliance repair shop, a grocery store, a furniture store, a barbershop and a tiny eatery. Tourists wouldn't frequent these businesses, island residents would. Danny and I had passed through here on our way to the national park.

Ryan parked the van on the wide dirt shoulder and led the way to a little building painted white. On the concrete slab in front of it were three round, white plastic tables, each with four plastic chairs. There was a window in the side of the small building for ordering. The menu and prices were hand printed in blue on a white board mounted next to the window. We were the only customers. Ryan ordered a cheeseburger, a bag of chips and a Diet Coke; I got a bottle of iced tea.

We sat at one of the tables. Ryan ate the chips and bought another bag. When his burger came, he devoured it, washing it down with gulps of his drink. Finally he said: "I couldn't sleep after I saw you last night and decided to look for Sara. I parked the van where they found her car and started walking. North first, then south and east. I searched till I was exhausted, then tried to sleep in the van for a couple of hours. At daybreak, I started looking again.

"This time I decided to search the abandoned North Shore Resort buildings. I found a body stuffed in a closet in one of the rooms."

"Sara?" I asked, horrified. "Oh no."

"Not Sara, Laurie."

"Laurie? Laurie's dead?" I was stunned.

"I called the cops on my cell phone. I've spent hours with them. They think I killed her."

"No word on Sara?" I asked.

Ryan looked miserable. "No. Karin has a lot of friends who own boats. Westwood thinks one of them gave Sara a ride to Curacao or Aruba, where she could fly back to the States."

"I talked to Karin less than an hour ago. She said she has no idea where Sara is. Even if she did, though, I don't think she would tell me."

Ryan put his head in hands and closed his eyes.

"This is a nightmare," he said. "Laurie's dead. Why would anyone kill her? And Sara's gone. I feel like a deer in the headlights. I don't know which way to turn, what to do."

"Sara wasn't happy here," I said.

"I know. She wasn't happy in California either. I don't think she'll ever be truly happy no matter where she lives. That's just the way she is. But I love my wife, negative attitude and all. I miss her terribly."

"You must have known having Laurie around was a reminder

you'd been unfaithful," I said. "Sara wanted you to fire her. Why didn't you?"

Ryan sighed. "Laurie loaned me money. I couldn't fire her."

"Did Sara know about this?"

"No. I was going to tell her, I just never got around to it.

"I thought I knew what I was getting into when I bought the inn. I was so naive. The previous owner had a loyal following and his customers returned year after year. Some stopped coming when he sold the SeaSide to me. More stopped coming when I raised the prices so I could make some upgrades.

"The improvements cost a lot more and took a lot longer than I expected. Nothing happens quickly on Bonamer. The rate hike didn't cover the costs. We had several expensive equipment failures. It was a struggle to make the mortgage payments.

"You already know Laurie and I had a one night stand. It happened when Sara went to the States to ask her family for more financial help. Instead of two weeks, she stayed a month. I was afraid she wasn't coming back.

"Laurie and I went out for a drink one evening after we closed the inn. We didn't stop at just one. Before long, I was telling her Sara was gone forever and I was probably going to lose the inn.

"Laurie offered to loan me the money she'd been saving to buy a new car. It wasn't a lot but enough to keep the SeaSide Inn afloat for a while. We celebrated by getting drunk and going to her place. I don't remember what happened next."

"Then Sara returned," I said. "Did her family come through with the money?

"No. They told her they couldn't afford to give us any more. They loaned us part of the down payment to buy the inn three years ago and we still haven't been able to repay any of it."

"You invited Danny here for a reason," I said. "What was that?"

"Is that what Danny thinks?"

"It's what I think," I said. "Danny thinks you're incredibly generous and enjoy his company."

Ryan sighed again. "I was hoping to convince Danny to sell his dive store and become a partner in the SeaSide Inn. He'd be such an asset. He can do just about anything and everyone loves him."

"He'd never move here, it's too far from Sam," I said. "Besides, he loves living in California and running Cliffview Divers."

Ryan gave me a bitter smile. "Yeah, well, it was worth a try. A desperate measure for a desperate man."

Chapter 26

We left the little café and climbed back in the van. I asked, "Could you show me where you found Laurie's body?"

Ryan frowned. "I'd rather not."

"You don't have to come with me. Just point me in the right direction."

"What the hell," Ryan said. "The day is a total loss anyway."

"Don't worry about your guests, most of them are diving with the GrapeTree, Danny and Weasel included.

"And here's something really strange: someone left the stolen laptop and video camera on our doorstep this morning."

Ryan didn't look at me. "At least there's some good news."

"You took them, didn't you? You didn't want the police to see the image and video I'd shot of the first time we found Van Slyke's body because it was anchored to the bottom with one of your fence posts. You didn't realize I'd have back-ups."

Ryan digested that for a few minutes. "I was really, really stupid," he said. "Does Danny know?"

"He knows I suspect you," I said. "He doesn't want to believe you'd do something like that. He idolizes you."

"At one time Sara thought I walked on water, too. Are you going to tell him?"

"No. You have to do that and deal with the consequences."

I changed the subject. "Did the police say how Laurie died?"

"I heard Westwood telling another cop it looked like blunt force trauma to the head. The top of her..." he stopped. "I'm sorry, I can't talk about it. It was awful to see her like that. I can't get that image out of my mind."

Tears filled his eyes and rolled down his cheeks. I quickly

looked away. We drove to the North Shore Resort in silence.

Just past the sign that read "North Shore Diving" Ryan parked the van and gestured to one of the rundown buildings. "She was in a room on the top floor. You won't have any trouble finding it, there's crime scene tape across the door."

The structure was quiet. Garbage littered the stairs to the second floor. All the windows had been broken and the rooms violently trashed. Doors were missing or hanging off their hinges. There were holes gouged in the walls.

Yellow tape crisscrossed an open doorway in the middle of the building. I ducked under it and went a few feet inside, following a path of footprints that led to a closet with no door. The way the dust was disturbed in the closet and the bloody smudges on one wall led me to believe Laurie's body had been propped up in a corner. It would not have been visible from the hall.

"Hey, didn't you see the tape?"

I jumped. I hadn't heard footsteps. Paul Metsalaer peered at me from behind the yellow tape. He wore brown surfer shorts, a beige tank top that showed off muscular arms, and sandals.

"Where was she?" I asked. "In that corner?"

"I didn't see her," Paul said. "Didn't want to."

"Did you or Les hear any unusual noises last night?"

"No."

"Westwood will have a fit." Les Gudrow joined Paul in the hallway. I hadn't heard him approach, either. "This is a crime scene you know."

I carefully retraced my footsteps.

"Did you see the body?" I asked Les.

He blinked and paled. "Yes."

"Was it in that corner?"

"Yes." Les had a distant look, as if he was seeing Laurie in his mind's eye.

"Was there a lot of blood?"

"A lot up here," Les answered, indicating his head and shoulders. "Look, I really don't want to discuss this. Laurie was my friend. It's hard to believe she died such a horrible death. She didn't deserve that."

"Where were you last night?" I asked.

"Not that it's any of your business, but Paul and I were together in the dive shop from 8:00 till 10:30. We got a shipment of new equipment yesterday, which we were pricing and shelving."

"Both of you?"

"Both of us," Les said firmly. "You really should go."

Paul regarded me blankly. "Bye," he said.

"See you," I said.

I walked down the hall. When I reached the stairs, I turned and glanced back. Paul and Les stood where I'd left them, watching me. I ran down the stairs.

Ryan sat under a tree near the van.

"Paul and Les find you?" he asked.

"They were in a hurry to get rid of me," I said. "I wonder why."

We got in the van and Ryan started the engine.

"How long did Paul work for you and why did you fire him?"

"He was with us three months. He had just moved here from Amsterdam. I fired him because I didn't like his attitude and discovered he was a substance abuser."

"Those aren't good attributes in an instructor."

"He isn't one anymore. I made sure of that. He has no professional rating of any kind, he simply goes along on trips to help Les, who is an instructor."

"Did Paul and Laurie date?"

"They were hot and heavy for several weeks but the relationship fizzled when she got to know him better. However, since they hung out at the beach bar they still ended up drinking together."

"Laurie's drinking didn't cause problems?"

"No. She's not, I mean wasn't, an alcoholic. She always showed up for work on time and sober."

The road to the SeaSide Inn took us past the marina. I looked for the *California Girl* but the big yacht was gone.

"I wonder if the Grahams found an instructor," I mused.

"If they hired someone local we'll hear about it," Ryan said darkly. "There are no secrets on Bonamer."

Chapter 27

The SeaSide Inn was very quiet when we returned and Ryan was able to slip into his home unnoticed. Before he did, he asked me if Danny, Weasel and I would help him run the boats and staff the shop. Of course I agreed.

I went upstairs, where I found a note from Danny: "Where the heck are you? We had a great dive, making another from the GrapeTree pier. Film at 5:00. L & K, Danny." Scrawled under that was "and Weasel."

Figuring there'd be a night dive, I got my camera system ready. Just as I finished, I heard the SeaSide Inn's compressor start up. Ryan was filling tanks.

Danny's note had piqued my interest. I decided to walk over to the GrapeTree. There, I sat on the edge of the pier and waited impatiently, watching bubbles I hoped were Danny and Weasel's on the water's surface. When the guys finally surfaced at the base of the ladder on the pier and saw me, they became positively giddy.

"You'll never guess what we saw, Sunshine." Danny handed me his camera, then his fins, and climbed up the ladder.

"You missed the best dive ever!" Weasel's fins and camera were entrusted to me as well.

"Wait till you see our footage!" they said simultaneously. They looked at each other and giggled. Ever heard grown men giggle? It's not pretty.

"What? Tell me," I demanded.

"Patience, patience," Weasel chided.

"Prepare to be absolutely green with envy," Danny teased.

My attempts to elicit more information were fruitless. I helped carry gear to the SeaSide Inn and suffered through the seemingly interminable gear rinsing and storing, during which the guys made irritatingly enigmatic comments to each other. Eventually, however, we gathered around the TV in our apartment. Danny fast-forwarded through the beginning of their first dive, then said, "Here it comes."

The video showed a school of grunts drifting lazily just above the sandy bottom.

"Hear that?" Danny asked.

There were squeaks and clicks in the distance. The camera swung upward, catching a huge dolphin upright and staring at the camera. The cetacean was about eight feet long and its streamlined body was a pale gray.

The animal remained motionless for a few seconds — a living sculpture — before turning and vanishing into the blue.

"That's fantastic," I said.

"Keep watching."

The dolphin repeated its performance two more times. On each occasion it hovered head up about 15 feet from Danny, its eyes fixed on the camera. Moments later, it was gone.

"Unbelievable," I said.

"Keep watching."

Squeaks and whistles were heard as a pod of at least 10 dolphins raced toward the camera. They circled it twice before speeding off out of sight.

"Let me show mine," Weasel begged. Although he hadn't filmed the solitary dolphin, he had gotten the pod. Both men were delirious with joy. I was, as Danny predicted, green with envy. It made me snappish.

"While you've been having fun, I've been dealing with another dead body," I said.

That got their attention.

"Oh no," Danny said. "Sara?"

"There's still no word on her. It's Laurie. Ryan found her body in one of the empty North Shore Resort buildings while he was searching for Sara. She was murdered."

Both men turned white. "Laurie?" Danny said. "Why would anyone kill Laurie?"

Weasel seemed incapable of speech.

I related the day's events, finishing with, "I told Ryan we'd help with the boats and the dive shop tomorrow."

"Of course we will," Danny said. "Laurie's dead and Sara's

missing. My God, what else can go wrong?"

A pall settled over us. Laurie had been a very special person and a lot of people would miss her. Who had killed her and why?

We had leftover chicken and coleslaw for dinner. We weren't really excited about making a dive that evening but figured we'd better. By tomorrow we wouldn't be on vacation, we'd be working.

The dive from the SeaSide Inn pier turned out to be a great diversion. Underwater, the day's events were forgotten. The highlight was the octopus I found. It was under a small rock, covered with algae and sponges, on the sandy seafloor. It was using an empty beer can as the door of its den. The octopus gripped the can with the suckers of one arm, peering out at us from beneath the long black spines of a sea urchin perched on the rock above it. Everyone had to photograph that unusual sight. We were talking and laughing about it as we climbed out of the water.

The return to reality didn't take long. Danny and I rinsed our camera systems and set them on towels on the kitchen table to dry. Then we went through our usual routine of downloading images and charging batteries even though Weasel was the only one who'd be taking photos in the morning.

Chapter 28

Sara had hitched a ride on the *California Girl* to Aruba. She hadn't wanted to go there and had no idea how she was going to explain the trip to Ryan.

It was all Paul's fault. He was so sure he'd get the instructor job on the Graham's boat that he had packed his bags before the interview. When Todd told him he'd have to pass a drug test and demanded a urine sample, Paul was furious. He stormed out of Todd's office and off the boat.

He was still seething when he called Sara. He said he couldn't afford a plane ticket to Aruba and Sara would have to go instead. The Grahams liked her and he was sure they'd be willing to give her a lift to Oranjestad.

Sara had gone there with a mission; sell the Cousteau book and get Paul out of her life. Their affair had to end, it just had to. It had become a miserable burden, filling up her head 24/7. She wanted it over. Selling the book would be her liberation. Paul had promised her a small share of the profits, which she would use to fly home to California. She didn't care where Paul went as long as it was far from her.

Sara's room in a really cheap motel didn't have a TV and she didn't find out there'd been a murder on Bonamer until she was having breakfast at a doughnut place and heard the American tourists at a nearby table discussing it.

She jumped up and went outside, where there was a newspaper vending machine. She didn't have the right coins and had to go back inside to get change.

Sara carried the paper to her table. While she was getting it, someone had cleaned the table and thrown her doughnut in the trash.

Luckily, she had taken her Diet Coke with her. She probably couldn't have eaten the doughnut anyway because her stomach was so roiled up.

She scanned the article on the newspaper's front page. It said Laurie was killed by a blow to the head and that Ryan had found her body while searching for Sara, who had gone missing.

Sara was stunned to learn that Laurie was dead. Why would anyone kill her? She had tons of friends. In fact, Sara was probably the only person on Bonamer who didn't like her.

The newspaper article speculated that Sara was also dead and her body would be found soon. Ryan was one of the few who thought she was still alive. Sara's eyes brimmed with tears when she read that Ryan had said: "I don't know where you are, Sara, or why you left, I only know that I want you back. Please come home. I love you and miss you."

Sara reconsidered her plans of moving to the U.S. Once the Cousteau book was sold, Paul would leave Bonamer forever. With any luck, she would never see him again, which was one huge problem solved.

Sara felt a little guilty when she realized she didn't have to worry about Laurie any more either. Maybe she should return to the SeaSide Inn, see if her marriage could be salvaged. Ryan didn't have to know about the affair with Paul or the stupid book. All she had to do was come up with a reason for her trip to Aruba.

Sara had contacted her mother and sister from an internet café shortly after she arrived on Aruba. She told them she had left Ryan and would be in California in a few days. She asked them not to tell anyone where she was. Now she really wanted to call or e-mail her husband. Better not. She had an appointment with the book dealer in the afternoon. She would have the money soon. She could decide what to do and where to go later.

Chapter 29

Time dragged in the dive store. I got my camera system ready for the afternoon dive. After that I swept the floor, then prowled the store, tidying up. The door to Ryan's office was camouflaged to look like part of the wall behind the counter and had a mask display on it. I was straightening one of the masks when I discovered the door was slightly ajar. It had been locked the other times I'd been alone in the store.

I pulled the door open and peered inside. Ryan's office was small and messy. The books in the shelves behind his desk appeared to have been stuffed in place hastily. On the floor were piles of paper, piles of magazines, and piles of piles. I went in.

I was surprised to see a couple of rebreathers in one corner. I couldn't remember Ryan mentioning that he owned any of these pricey underwater systems.

What caught my attention, however, was the computer that sat on Ryan's desk in the midst of several paper and book piles. There were no hot spots in the dive store, so I couldn't access the internet from my newly recovered laptop there, yet here was a computer sitting idle. A computer with an internet connection.

I felt a niggle of guilt, followed quickly by self-justification. Why shouldn't I use the computer? I didn't have anything else to do. If Ryan didn't like it, he could fire me. Fat chance of that.

I left the door open so I could hear the bell on the door if anyone entered the shop and jumped on the internet, going quickly to my e-mail. It had been a couple of days since I'd looked at it and there were quite a few messages, including two each from Dad and Sandy, along with eight from Danny's son, Sam, who often sent several at a time.

I read Sam's messages first. They were always short. I'd given him an inexpensive digital camera for his last birthday and he loved sending pictures. There were four photos of his twin siblings, two of his pet lizard and three of himself. I fired off quick replies and went to my stepmother's messages.

Sandy is a hugely successful real estate agent three months younger than I am. I had a little difficulty with her age — well, more than a little, actually — when I found out she and Dad were dating. Sandy was patient. She knew what she wanted and it didn't take long for her to win me over. She and Dad had my blessing when they married. And now, miracle of miracles, I had a six-month old half brother. Eight photos of him, captioned with clever sayings, were the reasons for Sandy's e-mails.

I replied with raves about the baby and opened Dad's messages. He had provided a rundown of the latest gossip in Cliffview and what was happening in his store, where Weasel and I also work. In my reply I told him about Sara's disappearance and Laurie's murder. When I clicked "Send" a new message appeared in my inbox from Captain Tony d'Argent, my supervisor at the Cliffview Police Department. While I truly love Danny, Tony is very attractive and has made it clear he'd be interested should I ever be available.

I opened his message half expecting an admission of how much he missed me. Tony, however, merely inquired when I'd be home so he could add me to the on-call schedule.

I said I wasn't sure and wrote an extensive account of what had happened on Bonamer. That took awhile. No one came into the shop so there were no interruptions. I finally sent the e-mail. When I closed the browser window, I noticed the icon for Apple mail in the dock at the bottom of the screen. I struggled with my conscience for at least five seconds before clicking on it.

As I had hoped, no password was needed for access. There were lots of messages, most from people I didn't know. As I perused the subject lines I saw an unread message with "Sara's Ok" on it. I opened it.

"Ryan," it read. "Sara contacted mom and me via e-mail. She is fine. Please don't try to find her. She has left Bonamer and won't be back. She said to tell you she hopes you and Laurie are very happy." It was signed, "Joanna."

I closed out the program. A quick glance at the clock told me the boats would be back from the morning dive soon. I positioned

Ryan's chair where I thought it had been when I entered the office and closed the door behind me. Then I sat on the stool behind the counter and wondered where Sara was. If she knew Laurie was dead would she change her mind about returning to Bonamer?

Chapter 30

Two days after she arrived on Aruba, Sara was on her way back to Bonamer. The book dealer had given *The Silent World* only a cursory glance before saying, "The book is only in good condition, not perfect, and there's no dust jacket." He opened the book and uttered an even worse appraisal. "The signature is a ghastly forgery. I can't believe anyone thought it was genuine. The book is worthless. Someone's made a fool of you."

Tears welled up in Sara's eyes and spilled down her cheeks. She began to sob.

The dealer was alarmed. He escorted her into his office, made her sit down and produced a glass of iced tea while he tried to calm her.

"There, there. Of course you couldn't know. But this isn't the end of the world. Life goes on. It's just a book."

Little did he know.

After a while, Sara took the book and left the store, not knowing what to do next. She didn't have enough cash or credit to buy a plane ticket to Miami. While there was enough for a ticket to Bonamer, Paul would still be there and she couldn't bear the thought of seeing him again.

She didn't e-mail Paul to tell him what she'd learned. When he didn't hear from her he would contact the dealer. He would know the bad news soon enough.

There was only one person who might help her with the plane fare and that was a long shot. Sara trudged to the internet café and e-mailed her sister, saying the money she had expected hadn't come through. She couldn't go back to Bonamer; she wanted to go home to her family. Could Joanna help her out one last time?

The reply came quickly. "We love you dearly, Sara, you know that," Joanna had written. "But none of us can afford to enable your financial irresponsibility any longer.

"You've only repaid half of what we loaned you to buy a car four years ago. Now that Mark's been laid off, we could really use that money.

"Don't bother asking Mom and Dad. You haven't repaid any of the loan they gave you to buy the SeaSide Inn. That was their retirement fund. Now they can't afford an RV and won't be doing any traveling.

"We all agree, no more loans. You need to start repaying what you owe us. A little every month is all we ask.

"We miss you. We'd love to have you nearby. But you have to stop living beyond your means and expecting us to bail you out when you fall short. Love, Joanna."

For the second time that day, Sara dissolved in tears. She and Ryan worked hard, it wasn't their fault the SeaSide Inn wasn't making a profit yet. How could her family desert her?

Sara walked the streets for several hours after that, weeping and thinking. The room she'd rented in the worst part of town was tiny and not very clean. She had underestimated how expensive it was to eat fast food, stay in even the cheapest motel and take taxis everywhere. Her supply of cash had dwindled even though she subsisted mainly on French fries and Diet Cokes. Soon, there would be only enough to get to the airport and buy a one-way ticket to Bonamer.

Sara dreaded going back to there. She couldn't imagine how Paul would react to having his dreams quashed. He hated having his father micro managing his life and now there was no end to that in sight. He would likely continue making her life hell unless she made a full confession to Ryan. Lord only knows how he'd take that news. Well, at least Laurie was no longer around to comfort him.

Chapter 31

Danny's face showed conflicting emotions when I told him I'd read Ryan's e-mail. He finally settled on a frown. "How could you do that?" he asked. "That's an incredible violation of Ryan's privacy."

"Don't ever try to keep anything from her," Weasel advised. "Her curiosity has no limits."

"I don't have any secrets," Danny said.

"My point exactly," Weasel agreed.

Danny frowned again.

"Look," I said. "While you may not like my methods, aren't you glad Sara's okay?"

Danny dodged that question with a stern warning, "Don't ever think of reading any of my mail without my permission. Not ever."

Anticipating good news from Ryan, we devoured our lunch and went downstairs well before the afternoon dive. Ryan was nowhere to be seen and the dive store was locked. We loaded tanks and our gear aboard the boats, then milled around in front of the sign-up board.

A few minutes after the boats were supposed to depart, Ryan came out of the dive store. He looked stressed yet all he said was, "Let's go. We're late."

I went out on Danny's boat. We had a good dive but as soon as I climbed back on board I began wondering what Ryan thought about the message he'd received. I would have bet the farm (if I had one) that he'd called Sara's sister during his lunch hour.

After the dive, Danny went to our apartment and I went into the dive store. Weasel and I were busy with customers till just after 5:00. Ryan remained in his office with the door closed.

When we were ready to leave for the day, Weasel yelled,

"Goodnight Ryan, see you tomorrow." There was no reply.

Back in our apartment, Danny looked at us expectantly.

"We didn't even see him," I said. "He never came out of his office. Why doesn't he tell us Sara's okay?"

"You're asking the wrong person, Sunshine."

We all felt a little down. We did camera maintenance and tried to figure out what to do about dinner. I opened the refrigerator and looked inside. "Half a dozen eggs, cheese, bagels, four energy bars and orange juice," I said. "We're almost out of beer. We need to go to the store."

"I'll fix an omelet," Weasel offered. "Tomorrow morning I'll ask Ryan if I can close the dive store for an hour and go shopping. You guys want anything, make me a list."

While Weasel whipped up what turned out to be a tasty omelet, I toasted and buttered bagels and Danny set the table. Our talk concerned what we'd done that day.

We were cleaning up when Weasel said, "We'll only be here a few more days. What will happen when we're gone? I'd stay if I could but school starts next week."

"I've got to get home, too," Danny said. "I've got a basic scuba class scheduled and Sam will be visiting me next weekend."

"Dad could probably manage without me, but I don't want to be here if you guys aren't," I said. "We'll have to remind Ryan we're leaving. He needs to hire a couple of people."

A thought struck me. "Did I mention that the *California Girl* was gone when we passed the marina yesterday?"

"I wonder if Todd found an instructor?" Weasel mused.

We looked at each other, one idea growing in three heads. I voiced it. "What do you want to bet he hired Sara? Her car was at the North Shore Resort, only a short walk from the *California Girl*."

"It should be easy enough to find out," Danny said. "I'll e-mail Todd."

While that should have been easy it wasn't. We could not get on the internet at any of our previous hot spots.

"The ISP is down," another laptop lugging guest advised as he departed. "It could be hours before it's up again."

"I'll try first thing in the morning," Danny said after several more unsuccessful attempts to connect.

He had good intentions. Unfortunately, he forgot to set the alarm. The compressor woke us. Danny jumped out of bed, pulled on swim trunks and ran down the stairs with Weasel on his heels. They filled tanks and loaded them onto the boats. I brought Danny a thermos of coffee and an energy bar to eat on the boat. Weasel took his breakfast into the dive shop.

I'd forgotten to sign up for Danny's boat and it was full, so I went out on Ryan's, which wasn't. I stood next to him at the wheel as he drove the boat to the site, making small talk and giving him plenty of opportunities to mention his sister-in-law's e-mail. He didn't, even when I asked, "Any news about Sara?"

Weasel did go grocery shopping while we were diving. Besides food, he brought back a copy of the Bonamer Current. It contained an article on Laurie's death that was illustrated with a recent candid photo of her and a photo of the pathologist arriving on Bonamer from Curacao via helicopter. Details were sparse and the results of the autopsy were not provided.

"This is so frustrating," I said. It had taken about ten seconds to read the article from start to finish and scrutinize the photos. "There's not really any news here."

Then I noticed a smaller article.

"Listen to this," I said: "Karin Van Slyke, Green Iguana Boutique owner, has moved to Holland, where she will marry her long-time beau, Hugo van der Mer, next week. After a honeymoon in Fiji, the couple will live in Amsterdam.

"This reporter ran into Karin at the airport yesterday, as she was checking in for her flight to the Netherlands. She said both the Green Iguana Boutique and her beachside condo are for sale. Those interested should contact Charlene at Bonamer Realty."

"Wow, that was quick," Danny said. "They've only been engaged a few days."

"She didn't mention moving or a wedding when I talked to her, what, 48 hours ago?" I pointed out.

Since I had to be in the dive shop that afternoon, I got Todd Graham's e-mail address from Danny. When the boats left, I would jump on the internet to ask Todd about Sara.

That didn't happen. Just after the boats departed, the bell over the door tinkled and two Dutch couples walked in. The women were new divers who wanted to buy dive computers. Each of the men, who were more experienced divers, recommended a different model. They all spoke very good English, but reverted to their native language when the discussion got heated.

They had looked at computers in several other dive stores on the island and the women were very confused. I took the computers out of Ryan's display case and set them on the counter.

The men got into a loud argument in Dutch. I motioned the women aside. "I think you'll like this one," I said. "It is easy to use and reasonably priced. It's compact. If you forget to turn it on before you go in the water, it turns itself on. You can change the batteries yourself, even in the middle of a diving day, and you won't lose any data. Let me show you how it works."

My presentation was finished in five minutes. "This computer can be programmed for nitrox if you ever decide to get certified to use it," I concluded. "You won't outgrow it. Best of all, I have two units in stock and you can have them right now. We take credit cards."

I was waiting for the credit cards to clear when the men realized something was afoot.

"Gentlemen," I said. "Are you familiar with this computer? It's the model I use. Let me show you why."

One of the men ended up buying a computer to use as a backup for his primary computer. While I was writing up his purchase, he asked if the SeaSide Inn made guests adhere to time and depth limits on their dives.

"I don't like surfacing while I've still got plenty of air in my tank," he grumbled. "The 45 minute dive time our resort tries to enforce is outrageous. We are paying to dive, let us dive. We know what we are doing, we are not going to get bent."

His friends murmured their assent.

"Divers are responsible for their own safety at the SeaSide Inn. Our philosophy is to let them do what they want to do, the owner doesn't believe in hand-holding," I said.

"What about nitrox and rebreather use?" his friend wanted to know.

"We can get nitrox tanks for you if you give us advanced notice and you can use whatever breathing system you wish."

"Do you have rebreathers for rent?"

Remembering the two units I had seen in Ryan's office, I said, "Let me check with the owner and I'll let you know." I wrote down his local phone number and told him I'd call him after I talked to Ryan.

When the shop was quiet again, I grabbed my laptop and went

to the pool. This time I was quickly connected to the web. I e-mailed Todd Graham, asking if Sara was on the boat and if so, would he please ask her to contact me. I went back in the shop. An hour later, I checked my e-mails. There was no reply.

I read and answered other e-mails, hoping a message from Todd would pop up on my screen. It didn't. No more customers came into the dive store either.

The boats finally returned. I couldn't ask Ryan if the rebreathers in his office were available for rent because I'd gone in there without his permission and shouldn't even know they existed. Instead, I told him two guests wanted to know if there was any place on the island where they could rent rebreathers.

"I'll get back to you," he said, then slipped into his office and closed the door.

Weasel and I handled a few minor sales, answered questions and checked in the two guests who had arrived on the afternoon flight from Amsterdam. At closing time, we yelled "good night" to Ryan. He did not reply.

Sitting on our balcony a while later, I checked my e-mails. There was still no message from Todd Graham.

Chapter 32

Dinner was barbecued pork chops and baked potatoes, with ice cream for dessert. Weasel presided over the grill and we ate at the big round table in the gazebo at the base of the SeaSide Inn pier. We'd decided against a night dive. We hoped Ryan would enlighten us about Sara's whereabouts and we wanted to make it easy for him to find us. I checked my e-mail hourly.

I finally got a reply from Todd Graham at 9:00 pm. The guys huddled around me while Danny read the most important part of it out loud.

"'Good to hear from you, Cinnamon. We gave Sara a ride to Aruba. She said she had business in Oranjestad and got off the boat there. We're surprised you didn't know. Is something wrong?'"

"Sara is probably in the U.S. by now," I said.

"Let's go see Ryan," Danny said.

The van was parked in front of the SeaSide Inn and there were lights on inside the Miller house yet Ryan did not answer the door. Danny knocked and yelled, "We aren't going away until you talk to us. Open up, we know you're in there."

The door swung open and Ryan stood there. He didn't look happy to see us.

"What do you want?"

"We know where Sara is, or at least, where she was yesterday," Danny said.

Ryan's anger evaporated. "Come in." He led us to the living room and said, "Where is she?"

Danny told him about Todd's e-mail. Ryan didn't say anything.

"You've heard from her, haven't you?" Danny asked.

"Not from Sara. I've had e-mails from and talked to her sister and mother. They said Sara was fine. They wouldn't tell me where she was."

"Do you think Van Slyke's death had anything to do with her leaving?" I asked.

There was a long silence. Finally Ryan said, "This has gone on way too long. Keeping Karin's secret has caused Sara and me a lot of problems. No more.

"Neils died in Karin's apartment and she panicked. After years of pretending she hated him the last thing she wanted anyone to find out was that they had never stopped seeing each other, which meant she couldn't call an ambulance to come get his body. Adding to her problem, Hugo was due in from Amsterdam in a few hours and she was supposed to pick him up at the airport and have dinner with him.

"Karin couldn't move Neils' by herself so she called Sara. The two of them put him in the trunk of her car."

Sara asked, "What am I supposed to do with him?"

Karin said: "As long as you take him as far away as possible from here I don't care."

"I was horrified that Sara not only agreed to help dispose of the body but involved me in doing so. I have no idea what she was thinking.

"I considered our options. Driving anywhere with a dead body in the trunk was out of the question. And, although we wanted it to be found quickly, we didn't want to be seen leaving it anywhere. This small island has very few places you can do anything without someone witnessing it, day or night.

"Although it was the easiest, we didn't want to dump the body in the water in front of our place. What if it washed up on our beach?" Ryan shuddered.

"Neils was a big man and we knew it was going to be difficult to move him. I finally decided the best solution was to load him into our inflatable from our beach and take him to the Town Pier. There were no ships docked at the pier that night. The inflatable is black and sits low the water. The engine on it is the quietest one we own. The trip up and back would take less than 10 minutes each way.

"I came up with the idea of tying the body to tires under the Town Pier and putting a No Tees hat on it. I thought it served Neils right. Sara wasn't happy about that, she thought Karin would be upset. I didn't care.

"We brought extra BCs to use as lift bags in case the body sank and that concrete fence post to keep it on the bottom if it floated.

"We saw the flashes of underwater strobes when we got to the Town Pier. We knew they were yours, Danny, because our van was parked in the lot next to the pier. When your lights went out, we knew you were headed toward shore, so I got into the water to look for a good place to put Van Slyke. That's when Sara decided to take matters into her own hands. She did not like being in a boat with a dead guy. She followed your bubbles and pushed the body out of the boat when she was on top of them.

"I couldn't believe she did that. I knew someone would recognize that fence post if we left it there. We had to move it before the police arrived."

Danny had been listening intently. Now there was skepticism on his face. "A couple of policemen were on the shore. They didn't see any regulator exhaust bubbles."

"We used rebreathers," Ryan explained. "We have two units. If I ever get the funds to buy more, I'm going to offer classes on how to use them, maybe even rent them."

Weasel had been as quiet as the proverbial mouse. Now he asked, "What the heck are rebreathers?"

"They're an alternative to scuba," Danny said. "There are no bubbles because the breathing gas is reused, not exhausted into the water after being inhaled as it is with the regulators we usually use."

"Exactly," Ryan said and continued his account. "After you went to get the cops we managed to move Neils and the fence post under the pier. Westwood would have found them if he'd looked there but he didn't. When everyone was gone, Sara used a lift bag to move the post to deeper water while I tied the body to the tires."

"We aren't criminals. Neils died a natural death. All we did was move his body. The police knew that as soon as the autopsy was done."

"Didn't you begin to wonder if Karin had lied, that maybe Neils' death wasn't natural?" I asked.

"You bet," Ryan said. "That was my first thought when the police showed up and carted us off to jail. It scared the hell out of me. Especially when they kept us overnight."

"You stole Cinnamon's laptop and my video to keep the police from finding out about the fence post, didn't you?" Danny asked.

"I'm sorry about that, Danny. It was dumb," Ryan admitted. "I didn't know you had copies."

"I thought Karin hated Neils," Weasel said. "What was he doing in her apartment?"

Ryan said: "Neils and Karin were lovers. They divorced because he wanted kids and she couldn't have any. He didn't want to adopt, he wanted biological children and thought using a surrogate was too risky. So he and Karin chose a woman they thought would produce suitable offspring. Neils and his second wife had two babies right away. He was supposed to divorce her and remarry Karin but he kept putting that off. Still, he and Karin remained close. To make sure no one suspected they were still seeing each other, Karin bad-mouthed him every chance she got."

"What about Hugo?" I asked. "The newspaper said he and Karin are getting married."

"Karin is a practical woman. Hugo was her insurance in case Neils never got around to divorcing his second wife. When he died she agreed to marry Hugo."

"Any idea who sent those e-mails to Sara about you having an affair with Laurie?" I asked.

Ryan shook his head. "None. I've printed them out, you can read them for yourself."

The first one he handed me, sent a few days before Danny, Weasel and I arrived on Bonamer, read: "Your beloved is screwing Laurie every chance he gets. Why do you put up with that?" It was signed, "Tattletale."

The second e-mail, sent a few days later, read: "Everyone knows what Laurie and Ryan do when they're alone together. Does he have anything left for you? Tattletale."

The third e-mail, sent the day before Neils Van Slyke died said: "Guess you don't care that your husband is f..... someone else. Are you really that much of a wimp?" It also came from "Tattletale."

"At first I thought Laurie sent those, hoping to break up my marriage," Ryan said. "That one night stand meant a lot more to her than it did to me."

"They don't sound like her," I said. "They're crude and cruel."

"Laurie didn't write those," Weasel said. "She's not mean."

"It had to be someone who knew about your one night stand with Laurie," Danny pointed out.

"Unfortunately, that wasn't a secret," Ryan said. "Laurie and I got drunk in a public place. Half the island knew we slept together that night, the rest learned about it the next day."

"These e-mails might be connected to Laurie's death. How can we find out who sent them?" I asked.

"Maybe the owner of the internet café in the mall can help," Ryan said. "He's a friend of mine. I think I introduced you to him at the No Tees meeting."

Danny, Weasel and I looked at each other blankly.

"There were a lot of people there," Danny said. "We don't remember him."

Chapter 33

Spending two or three hours underwater, combined with sea air and sun, is tiring. Most divers go to bed early. time we left Ryan's house, the lights were out in every SeaSide Inn apartment but ours. Weasel headed there immediately.

Danny and I walked out on the SeaSide Inn's short pier. It was a beautiful night with a crescent moon and a calm, silver sea. Danny's arms encircled my waist and drew me near. I rested my head on his chest. I felt very, very close to him.

"If I were Sara I wouldn't come back," I said. "Her two best friends treated her badly. She's better off without them."

Danny kissed the top of my head. "And how about Karin? Stringing Hugo along for years, then rushing to tie the knot before he finds out about Neils. Is that why you won't marry me? Do you have another lover stashed somewhere?"

I sighed dramatically. "Dozens of 'em. Good thing you've never looked under my bed."

"Oh, but I have," Danny said, "I helped you find an earring, remember? Any lover hiding under your bed risks certain death from noxious substances."

"I'm worth it," I said, kissing him.

"Prove it," Danny murmured, kissing me back.

It was a long, long kiss. I whispered, "Let's continue this discussion upstairs."

"Good idea."

As we turned toward shore, I saw something floating on the surface not far from the pier. It looked like a log — the kind of log that comes from a big tree. Only thing is, there aren't any big trees on Bonamer.

I peered at the object and pointed. "What is that?"

"It looks like a body," Danny said.

We ran to the beach and waded into the water. The body was only a few feet from shore. It was a man, wearing only a pair of red swim trunks. He was face down and Danny rolled him over on his back. When the moon illuminated his face, both of us gasped.

"Les Gudrow," I said.

Les' eyes were open and sightless.

"Let's get him up on the beach," Danny said.

We staggered ashore with Danny holding Les' head and shoulders and me his ankles. We laid the body on the sand. Danny checked for a pulse and breathing.

"He's gone," he said.

It was pretty obvious what killed him. One side of Les' head had been bashed in.

I left Danny on the beach and ran to Ryan's place. I had to pound on his door several times before he opened it. He was barefoot and wore only a pair of khaki shorts.

"Call the police. We just found Les Gudrow's body on the beach."

Ryan frowned as he processed that information. Then he brushed past me and jogged toward the pier. I called the police from the phone in his kitchen.

The officer who answered the call said nothing at all when I told him the news, he simply hung up the phone. I had no idea if that meant the police would be coming out or not.

Before joining Danny and Ryan I went to our apartment. Weasel was in the kitchen, drinking a glass of water when I burst through the door.

"What's going on?"

"Les Gudrow is dead." I grabbed my camera and strobe before dashing out the door with Weasel hot on my heels.

Danny and Ryan stood over the dead man. Ryan was agitated. "What is going on? First Laurie, now Les. Murders don't happen on Bonamer."

Falling back on my Cliffview PD training, I took photos. I was so engrossed in my work, I didn't realize the cops had arrived until Westwood grabbed my arm.

"What do you think you're doing?"

"I'm a forensic photographer. I'm taking photos of the body for you. Tell me what you want me to do."

Westwood assessed the idea. "Wait here," he said. "Don't move." He conferred briefly with the two other officers before asking, "Is this where you found him?"

"No," I said. "He was face down in the water beside the pier. We brought him up on the beach."

"You should have left him where he was," Westwood complained.

"We didn't know if he was alive or dead till we got him on land."

Westwood approached the body and examined it with a powerful flashlight. After giving his men orders to secure a large area with crime scene tape and search it for possible clues, he gestured to me. Following his brusque commands, I took numerous photos. Most of them were repeats of shots I'd already taken.

By the time I finished, the rest of the SeaSide Inn's guests had gathered on the porch that was directly under the oceanfront balcony of our apartment. Guests from the GrapeTree had noticed the commotion and shown up to see what was happening as well.

We all watched Les' body being zipped into a body bag and carried to an ambulance. Westwood said, "That's all folks. Go back to bed."

To me, he said, "Let's go upstairs."

As Weasel and Danny watched, Westwood directed me to download the images from my camera to my laptop and burn them onto the two DVDs he'd brought, which I did.

"Now move the photos to the trash," Westwood directed with a smirk, "and empty it."

I did as commanded. He took the DVDs and left without bothering to say "thanks."

From the kitchen balcony, we watched all but two of the cops pile into their cars and drive off.

Weasel broke into a grin. "Pretty crafty, Cin. Westwood thinks he has the only copies of those photos but they're still on the memory card in your camera."

"Yes," I said. "I would have deleted them if he'd asked. Did you see the look on his face when he told me to empty the trash on my laptop? What a jerk."

"Why do you want photos of a dead man?" Danny asked. "Wasn't seeing him enough?"

"I only kept them because Westwood made me mad," I said. "Don't you find him irritating?"

After uploading the images to Dad's website, I deleted them from the memory card and the laptop. It was possible someone would point out his mistake to Westwood and he'd be back.

Meanwhile, Weasel checked the doors and windows and wandered off to bed. Danny rechecked everything, then went to our room.

I, too, made the rounds, making sure everything was locked up tight. I noticed one patrol car remained in the SeaSide Inn lot and there were two cops searching the shallow water off our oceanfront balcony. The police were looking for clues where we first saw the body.

I brushed my teeth, washed my face and slipped under the sheets with Danny, who didn't even notice. A new day was dawning before I finally fell asleep.

Chapter 34

The sound of the compressor awoke me long before I was ready. I was bleary-eyed and sluggish from lack of sleep. Since it was my turn to staff the dive shop I somehow summoned the energy to slip into a swimsuit, shorts and flip-flops. I drank three cups of coffee.

Shortly after the boats left for the morning dive, I had an inspiration. I ran upstairs and got my laptop. Under a palm tree poolside, I e-mailed dad and asked him to make eight by ten inch prints of three of the images I'd left on his website and take them to Tony d'Argent at the Cliffview PD as soon as possible. I told him to ask Tony to e-mail me when he got them.

I returned to the dive shop. While I only intended to close my eyes for ten minutes, when I put my head down on the counter I fell asleep.

The tinkle of the bell on the door awakened me. I rubbed my eyes and looked up. Westwood and another Bonamer police officer stood in front of me.

"You have copies, don't you?" Westwood looked angry.

"What are you talking about?" I asked, though I was pretty sure I knew.

"The photos you took of Les Gudrow's body. They are still in your camera, aren't they?"

"No," I said. "I deleted them from the memory card."

"You don't have copies on your laptop?" the other officer asked.

"No," I said, summoning indignation. "I don't have any copies of the photos I took last night in my camera, laptop, CD, DVD or portable storage device."

Westwood and the other officer retired to a corner of the shop and conferred. As they left Westwood said, "We might be back."

When the boats returned from the morning dive, I walked down to the pier to meet them. Something was very wrong. No smiling, happy faces greeted me. There was no chatter or banter about what had been seen or done on the dive. People averted their eyes as they got off the boats and Ryan went straight to the dive shop without saying a word.

Guests gathered around the sign-up board. I watched as they erased their numbers on the list for the afternoon boat, then began returning the weights and/or weightbelts they'd been issued when they checked into the inn at the beginning of their vacations.

I was shocked. None of these people were scheduled to check out today but that was what they were doing. When I tried to ask Danny what was going on he said, "Not now, Cinnamon. I'm sure Ryan and Weasel could use your help in the shop."

He was right. The dive shop was crowded. I was pressed into service, settling accounts and processing payments.

Ryan told us to charge only for actual days of diving and room occupancy, not what had been reserved. Though his face showed the strain, he remained calm and polite.

The guests were apologetic, saying they no longer felt safe staying here now that two people had been murdered on the island, one of them on the beach right in front of the inn.

In order to take care of everyone, the dive shop stayed open through the lunch hour and the afternoon boat left the dock an hour late. Ryan had asked Danny to run it and said he'd staff the dive shop so Weasel and I could dive. We thought that would be detrimental to Ryan's mental health. We insisted he go out on the boat.

Though it was Weasel's turn to staff the dive shop, I volunteered, hoping to hear from Tony. Weasel didn't object. He was happy to go diving with Danny, Ryan and the four guests who had decided to stay.

Danny, however, looked at me as if I had lost my mind.

"I need to answer e-mails," I explained. "There are four from your son alone and you know how disappointed he is when he doesn't hear back from us right away. You answered yours yesterday."

"Right," Danny said, not deceived. "You're giving up a dive to answer e-mails?"

"That's part of it, yes. I'll tell you all about it later."

"You better not be snooping into the murders," Danny said. "That would be dangerous."

The guys grabbed energy bars, apples and bottled water to eat on the boat. I fixed a sandwich and took it to the shop. Departing guests passed the front door continually. It was very depressing. Before long, the resort would be a ghost town.

I took the laptop out to the pool and got on the internet. Although it's supposed to be high speed, Bonamer's ISP gives new meaning to the term, "slow connection." While I waited, I remembered the messages Sara had received from "Tattletale" and realized we'd never told the police Sara wasn't really missing. They needed to know the search was off. I'd remind Ryan to call Westwood when the boat returned.

I wondered anew who Todd Graham had interviewed for the *California Girl* job and if he'd hired someone. I e-mailed him and was pleased when his reply popped up in my inbox almost immediately.

"Hi Cinnamon," it read. "I hired Jason. Do you know him? He worked at the GrapeTree. I talked to one other instructor and had an interview scheduled with Laurie. She never showed up. We were really disappointed about that. She was our number one choice after Danny.

"How's the weather there? We are on our way to a rainy Belize."

My message said: "Thanks for your prompt reply. I have bad news about Laurie. She was murdered; probably on the night she had the appointment with you. The police don't seem to have any suspects. Who was the third person you interviewed?"

Again, the answer came immediately. "Laurie? Murdered? How horrible! She was a wonderful young woman. Please keep us up to date on the investigation.

"Oh yes — the third instructor was from North Shore Diving. I liked the GrapeTree guy better."

After reading Todd's last message I answered e-mails from Sandy, Sam, assorted friends and Greene's customers. By the time I finished, there was a new e-mail from Dad:

"Wished you'd warned me about those photos," he wrote. "I wasn't prepared for images of a dead man. I hope he wasn't a friend of yours. Isn't this the third body you've found on Bonamer? Sandy and I are extremely worried. We think all of you should come home immediately."

The e-mail continued. "Tony has the prints."

I e-mailed an apology to Dad and sent Tony a message, asking if he could find out what caused the injury to Les' head. I was glad California was three hours behind us; although it was 2:00 pm on Bonamer, it was only 11:00 am in Cliffview.

My luck held. Tony replied, "I'll show the photos to the pathologist tomorrow morning. I have to see her about something else anyway." He added, "Don't get involved in any murders down there, Cinnamon. Let local law enforcement handle them. You're a valuable employee and we don't want anything to happen to you. Even the chief misses you. Just yesterday he asked when you're coming home. Stay safe. Tony."

That made me smile. I very much doubted that Chief of Police John Lawson anxiously awaited my return. Our relationship had soured one Halloween when I was a senior in high school and he was a Cliffview PD rookie. Most likely he was hoping I'd become a permanent resident of Bonamer.

I logged off and closed the laptop.

Just before the boats returned a woman came into the shop. About my height, she was in her late 50s, with short, silver-blond hair and green eyes. She had fair skin and a sprinkling of freckles across her nose.

"Hello, I was wondering if you had any vacancies." Her eyes searched my face so intensely I was startled and took a step backward.

"You're in luck. We've had some cancellations," I said, trying not to seem too eager. "We've got a really nice suite with bedroom, living room and kitchenette, as well as a couple of single rooms with toaster, microwave and small refrigerator. How many people will be checking in?"

"Just me. The suite sounds great."

"What kind of package are you interested in? We have boat dives, beach dives or a combination of both. I recommend the combo."

"Oh, I'm not a diver, though I might try snorkeling."

"You can do that right off our beach or pier," I said. "We even have snorkeling gear for sale or rental. How long will you be staying?"

"Is the suite available for five days?"

"I'll check," I said, knowing that of course it was. The SeaSide Inn had four suites available, all vacated that morning. I flipped through a book pretending to be looking for something. The woman didn't need to know I wasn't checking reservations, which were stored in the computer in Ryan's locked office. "The suite is yours," I told her.

She seemed delighted and smiled at me, revealing a network of fine lines around her eyes and mouth. Something about her was very familiar. "Have we met before?" I asked.

"Anything is possible," she said. "Can you put the charges on my Visa?"

The woman's name was Julie Wade. When all the paperwork was completed, I handed her the key to the suite and watched her walk out the door. Looking at her slim body, I revised my estimate of her age. She was younger than I'd thought. I'd bet she hadn't had an easy life.

Chapter 35

That night we decided to go into town for a pizza dinner. We invited Ryan to come with us. He declined, saying he wanted to spend some time alone. That he would be able to do; the SeaSide Inn was nearly deserted. I reminded him to tell Westwood that Sara had contacted her family. Danny reminded him that we'd be going home in a few days and he needed to hire people to take our places.

"Unless more customers show up, I won't need anybody else, I'll be able to run the place all by myself," he replied.

As Danny, Weasel and I walked to the mall, they told me what had happened that morning.

"The guests started talking about Les' murder on the way to the dive site," Danny said. "They thought he was killed at the SeaSide Inn and were terrified. After the body was discovered, half of them spent the rest of the night at the GrapeTree. Those who stayed at the SeaSide didn't get much sleep. Most of them are moving somewhere else for the last few days of their vacations. They were only here this morning to make a last dive and check out."

I said: "I don't think Les was bludgeoned to death on the SeaSide's beach or pier. Westwood had me photograph both and we didn't find any blood. I think Les was killed elsewhere and his body was put in the ocean near the inn's beach."

"Still, two people have been murdered and strange things happened to the body of another," Weasel said. "Everyone's afraid they'll be the next victim."

"This is a disaster for Bonamer and the SeaSide Inn," Danny said. "If the police don't solve the murders soon there won't be a tourist left on the island."

He was right. When we passed the Town Pier only a few people were getting ready to go into the water.

That reminded me of my internet chat with the owner of *California Girl*. "I had a couple of e-mails from Todd Graham today," I said. "I asked who interviewed for his job. He said there was an instructor from North Shore and Jason from The GrapeTree. He hired Jason. Laurie was his first choice but she didn't show up for her interview. I told him she was probably killed before she could."

"Did he say whether it was Les or Paul from North Shore?" Danny asked.

I shrugged. "I assumed it was Les. Ryan told me Paul lost his instructor certification."

"The Grahams might not know that," Danny pointed out.

"Why did you offer to stay in the dive shop this afternoon?" Weasel asked me.

I told the guys about the photos I'd asked Dad to print and take to the Cliffview PD. "I should hear back by tomorrow.

"Did I mention that Westwood brought another officer to the dive shop this morning and accused me of keeping copies of the photos I shot last night?"

Danny and Weasel exchanged meaningful glances. "Imagine that," Weasel said.

"I told them I didn't have any," I said. "It was the truth. After I uploaded them to Dad's website, I deleted them from my camera and laptop."

We ordered an extra large pepperoni pizza and a pitcher of beer. We hadn't discussed making a night dive but everyone knew we wouldn't. Les' body had been found not far from where we usually entered the water. That made me more than a little uneasy; I'm sure Danny and Weasel felt the same way.

The guys knew about Julie, who had checked in while they were out on the boats. When I saw her ordering food, I waved to her. She came over to our table, holding a soft drink.

"Come join us," I said and introduced her to Danny and Weasel.

After she settled down at our table, I said, "If you're not a diver, why did you come to Bonamer? Are you a birdwatcher?"

Julie took a long sip of her drink before answering, "Isn't the island's natural, unspoiled beauty reason enough?" She smiled.

Weasel tried next. "Where do you live in California?"

"Oakland," Julie said, taking another long sip. We waited for more but more wasn't forthcoming.

"Are you a California native?" That was Danny's attempt to start a conversation with the stranger.

"No," Julie said.

Silence descended as our pizza arrived and we gave it our full attention. Ordinarily, the bar on the other side of the street was crowded and noisy. Tonight only a few people had gathered there and the chatter was subdued. Being in the mall overlooking that bar and the harbor made me realize how much had changed in the past few days. Les and Laurie were dead; Sara and Karin had fled the island.

Weasel took the last slice of pizza and voiced a fear we all shared. "Do you think we'll be safe at the inn tonight?"

"I hope so," Danny answered.

"We shouldn't have any trouble if we stay together and make sure all the doors and windows are locked when we go to bed," I said.

Julie looked alarmed. "I've heard people talking about the murders. Do you think I'll be okay in my place?"

"If you're worried you can sleep on our couch tonight," Weasel offered. "We've got plenty of room."

"Thanks, I may take you up on that."

We stood in a short line to get ice cream cones before making our way back to the SeaSide Inn. The sun was long gone.

"Is it my imagination or are there fewer people out this evening?" Weasel asked.

"I was thinking that, too," I said.

"Everyone's a little spooked," Danny said.

At the inn, there was more bad news. Two of the four people who'd planned to stay had changed their minds. Long-time customers, they'd been vacationing at the inn for nearly two decades. They were stuffing suitcases into their rental car as we walked up.

"We hate to do this to Ryan but we wouldn't sleep if we stayed," the woman told us. "We're moving to the Green Iguana for our last two nights."

That left Danny, Weasel, me, Ryan and Julie, along with two other guests, Mike and his wife Vicky.

"I'll come up about 9:30, if that's okay," Julie said. Her suite was across the pool from ours.

As Danny, Weasel and I sat around the kitchen table working on our cameras I asked, "Does Julie look familiar to you? I keep thinking I've met her before."

"Me, too," Danny said.

"Me three," Weasel chimed in. "She seems nice though she certainly is secretive. Even Cinnamon failed to extract info from her."

When Julie showed up with a set of sheets and a pillow, I showed her the couch and pointed out the bathroom. "Make yourself at home."

"Thanks, Cinnamon, I really appreciate this." She smiled. Her eyes lingered on my face so long I wondered what she was seeing there.

"No problem," I said. "I wouldn't want to spend the night alone either."

At bedtime, Weasel made the rounds, closing and locking windows and doors. Danny rechecked everything. While he brushed his teeth, I did my own reconnaissance.

Though I was really tired, I couldn't sleep. Every time a tree branch rustled or the breeze sent leaves awhirl on the ground I was instantly alert, my heart in my throat.

After a restless hour, I decided to check the windows and doors one more time. I crept from the bedroom, closing the door quietly behind me. While there was enough light to navigate without crashing into things, there wasn't enough to make sure the windows were locked. Weasel's dive light was on the kitchen table, so I used it.

I had confirmed that all the windows and doors were secure in the kitchen and was tiptoeing toward the living room when I saw a cockroach on the floor. I don't like roaches. The Bonamer versions, several times larger than their California cousins, are especially repugnant. They are also considerably bolder. This one didn't run; it lingered in the spotlight, antennae twitching.

The idea of stomping on the inch and half long insect was disgusting. I didn't want a smelly mess on the bottom of my flip-flop. Worse, what if I wasn't able to kill it and it ran up my leg? I shuddered.

There was a can of bug spray under the kitchen sink. I'd dispatched several roaches with it since we'd been here. The bugs were so big they required multiple sprays before turning turtle and giving up the ghost.

While I was retrieving the spray, the huge roach scuttled off somewhere. Light in one hand, spray can in the other, I searched for it.

Then I heard a key in the kitchen door. I turned toward the sound just as the door popped open. It hit the wall with a bang.

"Hands up, don't move!" came the order. The beam shining in my eyes blinded me.

My arms shot up. The can of roach spray flew out of my hand and hit a wall before dropping onto the ceramic tile floor with a clatter. It bounced and rolled, coming to a stop against a chair leg.

The kitchen light came on. Ryan stood in the doorway, an aluminum baseball bat in his upraised hand.

The bedroom door sprang open. Danny stood there, the lamp from our bedside table in one hand, its cord dragging on the floor. The door to Weasel's room opened a crack and he peered out. Julie appeared in the living room doorway, her face white.

For at least two minutes all of us stared at each other. Danny broke the silence.

"What the hell is going on?"

"I couldn't sleep," I explained. "I was checking the locks on the doors and windows when I saw a roach. I got the can of bug spray and was looking for it when Ryan barged in."

"I couldn't sleep either," Ryan said. "I was sitting on the pool deck when I saw a light moving around in your kitchen. I was sure there was a burglar, or worse, in here." He leaned the baseball bat against the doorframe.

Two Bonamer policemen appeared behind him. "What's the problem?" one of them asked.

Before everything got sorted out, the other two SeaSide guests, Mike and Vicky, were awakened by the commotion and showed up to find out what was happening.

The cops departed as soon as they found out everyone was okay. I handed out our last beers. When those were gone, Mike and Vicky made a trip to their place, returning with a couple of six packs and some snacks. The popcorn, prepared in our microwave, tasted especially good.

After a second beer, I slunk off to bed and fell asleep. I don't know when Danny joined me; I was truly dead to the world. I didn't know Ryan, Mike and Vicky had spent the night in our apartment until I dragged myself out of bed the next morning and found bodies, live ones this time, everywhere.

Chapter 36

I picked my way to the kitchen, where I made coffee. I took a cup of it out on the balcony that overlooked the ocean. Mike and Vicky had moved the couch that was usually out there into the living room and were sound asleep on it. Julie slept nearby.

I sat on one of the chairs on the balcony, admiring yet another of Bonamer's perfect days. It was still and peaceful, the sun bright in a powder blue sky accented with fluffy white clouds. A slight breeze ruffled the clear turquoise sea.

A boat pulled up to The GrapeTree's pier, loaded a dozen divers on board and headed north. I found myself wishing I was on that boat and not at the SeaSide Inn with six other frightened people.

I was glad I hadn't tried to wrestle with the "intruder" in the dark. If I had, Ryan might have have beaned me with the bat.

That made me think of the other baseball bat I'd seen on the island; the one Paul and Les used to kill cockroaches. A shiver ran down my spine as I remembered how Les had squashed the roach in his shop.

Julie appeared while I was thinking about that. When she saw my cup, she went back inside and returned with a cup of her own. She sat down in the chair next to mine.

"That was one of the most eventful evenings I've had recently," she said. "I'll never forget seeing Ryan holding that bat, ready to beat somebody's brains out."

Weasel wandered out on the balcony with a cup of coffee. His eyes were at half-mast.

"How late did you stay up last night?" I asked.

He shook his head. "I didn't look at the clock when Ryan and I went to bed but it wasn't that long ago."

Just then Ryan stumbled out, noticed our cups, sniffed the air and went back in. Danny showed up next. He confiscated my cup and drained it, then went inside to refill it.

Ryan returned, trailed by Mike and Vicky. The three of them dragged the sofa out on the balcony and settled on it with their coffees.

Vicky looked from me to Julie, then Julie to me. "Are you related? You look like sisters," she said. "One blond, one redheaded."

That caused everyone to scrutinize us. Julie stiffened.

"I don't have a sister," I said. "But if I did, she might look like you. It's weird that we look alike. It's even weirder that my mother's name was Julie."

"I don't have a sister, either," Julie said, her voice faint.

"The two of you do look alike," Weasel said. "Same shaped face and nose, same build. It's uncanny."

"Did your mother have a sister?" Vicky asked Julie.

"No."

"Where were you born?" I asked.

"The Midwest," Julie said, peering into her cup.

"Wisconsin by any chance? That's where my parents grew up."

Julie sat very still and didn't look up. "Yes."

"Maybe you two are long lost cousins," Vicky said.

Julie stood up abruptly. "Excuse me. I need more coffee." She headed for the kitchen.

Ryan asked, "Anybody want to go diving?"

Of course we did.

"Since this is Mike and Vicky's last day, they get to choose the site," Ryan said. "No point in keeping the dive store open, there won't be any customers. We can all go."

As Julie reappeared, Ryan added, "You're welcome to join us."

"I think I'll stay here and do some reading," Julie said. "There's a really nice breeze on the pool deck. Thanks anyway."

Ryan continued. "What the heck, the day is already screwed up. Bring food and water. We'll make two dives and have lunch on the boat in between them. It's late, let's hustle."

That we did. Danny and Weasel loaded the boat with tanks for two dives while I filled a cooler with the contents of our refrigerator: cheese, crackers, oranges and bottled water. We schlepped cameras and gear to the boat and got in.

All the activity raised the spirits of our little group. It was good to be underway. The noise from the outboards and the water rushing past the hull made talk nearly impossible and I had time to think.

Julie looked so much like me and remembering how intensely she had scrutinized my face the first time we met, I'd bet she knew why. I, however, had no clue. Both sets of Minnesota grandparents had died when I was young and I barely knew them. Neither of my parents had siblings. There must be relatives somewhere but if so, I'd never met them. I'd have to ask dad when I got home.

The trip to the dive site took more time than usual. Mike and Vicky had requested Red Slave Huts, at the far southern end of the island. We'd dived the site with Laurie earlier in our stay and found it outstanding.

That thought saddened me. I'd liked Laurie a lot and I missed her. She was a nice person and a terrific dive buddy/critter finder. I wondered if the SeaSide Inn could survive without her.

I glanced at Ryan now, as lost in his thoughts as I was in mine. Now that I'd seen him, bat raised and ready to defend us, I knew Danny was right. He was friend, not foe. I couldn't imagine him killing Laurie or Les.

So who killed Laurie and why? Did the same person murder Les? Did we know the real reason Sara went away? Where was she?

After awhile, I gave up trying to answer those questions and just enjoyed being out on the water. We would be going home soon and there wouldn't be many more Bonamer dives.

The boat's progress caused a steady stream of flying fish to jump into the air and skitter across the surface. Weasel started timing how long each stayed in the air and announcing it.

"Ten seconds!"

"Fifteen seconds. That was a champion!"

"Twenty-five seconds. I think we have a winner!" Danny shouted.

At Red Slave Huts, we decided to dive as a group, with Ryan as our leader. I expected him and Danny to kick into macho mode and leave the rest of us behind. Instead, Ryan headed south at a leisurely pace. He searched cracks and crevices, pointing out a moray, a huge lobster and a variety of small critters. He also found a black seahorse.

Vicky was also an excellent creature finder. Her sharp eyes

discovered a couple of mating sea slugs called nudibranchs, an unusual blenny and a rare fingerprint flamingo tongue shell. Danny, Weasel, Mike and I were kept busy shooting stills and video.

One of the things I love about diving is that it makes you focus on the moment. Problems are forgotten.

We surfaced, laughing and joking. As we ate lunch on the boat I asked Ryan, "Do you ever dive the east coast?"

"Occasionally. There's only one mooring there, at a site called White Hole. It's an underwater sinkhole about 50 feet deep with a white sand bottom, roughly the size and shape of a football field. A school of tarpon hangs around the southern end, there's a humungous green moray in a small cave and a shallow cavern full of silversides. At night we've seen some really big spiny lobsters and a variety of slipper lobsters."

"Sounds great," Danny said. "Why don't you go there on a regular basis?"

"It's four hours roundtrip by boat and the ocean is usually rough on that side," Ryan said. "We tried putting the boat on a trailer and launching it over there but it's still a hassle. And diving this side of the island is so easy."

"Still, the reefs must be pristine and there must be animals you won't see here," Mike said.

"That's true," Ryan admitted. "Sara, Laurie and I did an exploratory trip a couple of years ago. There are reasons why so few operators go there. For one thing, Conch Bay is the only place you can launch a boat.

"What about the beaches at the island's north end? Danny and I looked at a couple in the national park," I said.

"The surf's too big and there's no ramp. The car and the trailer would get stuck in the sand. Besides, even the closest beach in the park is a 90 minute drive from the SeaSide Inn," Danny replied.

"Right," Ryan said. "Plus there aren't any moorings. It's illegal to anchor a boat anywhere in the marine park, which includes all the waters surrounding Bonamer and Little Bonamer down to 200 feet. That means you have to do a live boat drift dive. You drop your divers in the water and follow their bubbles on the surface so you're there when they come up.

"The day we dived the east coast the current was really ripping, running north at least two knots. That's impossible to swim against. I wouldn't run regular trips there even if the access was easier. The conditions are too dangerous for most divers.

"Of course, since no one goes there the reefs are really nice and you do see bigger animals. We saw a lot of turtles and several eagle rays. Oh, and two sharks."

"Sharks?" Weasel was immediately alert.

"I don't know what kind," Ryan said. "They didn't come close and left when they saw us."

Ryan moved the boat to Pink Beach for our second dive. The site is so named because the sandy shore is pale pink. This time we split up. Ryan went off on his own, Mike and Vicky did their thing, and Weasel, Danny and I were once again a threesome.

It was an above average site. The most interesting find was a lionfish. Two species of these fishes, natives of the tropical Pacific, were first found in the Atlantic Ocean off Florida in 1985. It is thought they were aquarium fish released by someone who had no idea how quickly their numbers would grow in predator free waters. The fish had already spread to the Bahamas and now Bonamer had them, too. Lionfish have voracious appetites everyone worried about their impact on local fish populations.

Lionfish are, however, beautiful and we photographed the one we found. The fish usually face away from the camera, relying on their venomous spines to protect them, and this one was no exception.

The long trip back to the SeaSide Inn was made in relative silence. Our brief respite from murder was about to end.

Chapter 37

The return to the Inn was more traumatic than anyone expected. Westwood and another officer awaited us. As soon as the boat was tied up, they escorted Ryan to the dive store and disappeared inside.

The rest of us unloaded the tanks and washed the boat, then rinsed our gear and put it in our lockers. Danny and Weasel began filling empty tanks; I went up to our apartment. There, I showered and began my camera maintenance ritual, frequently interrupted by trips to the balcony to see what was going on below.

The officer who'd come with Westwood made several trips to his patrol car, parked at the SeaSide Inn's entrance. He carried paper bags and part of Ryan's computer, which he put in the trunk.

I gave up trying to work on my camera; I just couldn't concentrate. I took the laptop to the pool area and jumped on the internet. When I glanced up, I could see what was going on.

My e-mail inbox contained a message from Cliffview PD. I'd almost forgotten about the photos I'd had dad give Tony d'Argent.

"You know, of course, that the pathologist can't provide a definitive answer without examining the body," Tony wrote. "She says, however, that she's seen similar wounds caused by a baseball bat. That could (emphasis on could) be the weapon in this case. Hope this helps. See you soon."

I had just finished reading that message when the police ushered Ryan out of the dive shop. He handed the SeaSide Inn keys to Danny.

"Take care of things," he said. "I don't know when I'll be back."

The cops put him in the patrol car and drove off. "What did they want?" I asked.

"I don't know," Danny said. "But they took Ryan's baseball bat.

Why would they want that?"

"Tony just e-mailed me that Les Gudrow may have been killed with a baseball bat," I said. "The cops saw Ryan with one last night."

"Not that he would have but Ryan couldn't have killed Les," Danny pointed out. "We were with him when that happened."

"We were with him part of the evening," I said. "We don't know where he was from the time the boats docked in the afternoon until we went to his house after dinner. But I don't think he's the killer either."

Chapter 38

We discussed how to run the Inn without Ryan over a dinner of peanut butter sandwiches in the gazebo, where Mike and Vicky joined us. We wondered where Julie was; we hadn't seen her since morning.

"Ryan told me several guests cancelled," Danny said. "Those who didn't will arrive tomorrow. I have no idea what rooms to put them in. All that information is in the computer, which the police took."

"If they're repeat guests, like we are, they probably requested specific units," Mike said. He and his wife were long time SeaSide customers. "All you have to do is ask them. Others may have reserved a certain type of unit. You know, one bedroom, studio, etc. They should have the confirmation letter Sara sent them. It will say what unit they were assigned.

"Most people don't expect to make a boat dive the day they arrive. They want to unpack and settle in. Just make sure there are tanks available in case someone wants to make a dive off the pier."

"Weasel and I know how to check people in and run the shop, Danny," I pointed out. "You know how to fill tanks, issue weights and weightbelts and run the boats. We'll manage somehow."

Although we didn't see Mike and Vicky early the next morning, we knew they had to pack and get ready for their trip home. We were concerned about Julie, though. Danny knocked on the door of her apartment, then disappeared inside.

"She's fine," he told me a few minutes later. "Said she just wants to be a hermit for awhile."

"Did you notice how nervous she got when everyone started

looking at her yesterday?"

"She definitely wasn't happy about that," he agreed.

We didn't have time to think about this, we were too busy. Four couples with a total of three kids arrived on the morning flight. Most were repeat customers and knew which units they had rented. When they found out Ryan was in jail, they expressed concern. We assured them he was innocent and would soon be back at the inn. Until then, we would make sure they got the vacation they expected.

There were only nine divers so only one boat was needed in the am. Weasel staffed the shop, I would do it in the afternoon.

The three of us were supposed to be on a plane headed for the States in two days. We needed to extend our stay. I planned to spend my afternoon in the shop re-booking our flights and notifying our nearest and dearest. I also wanted to take the "Tattletale" e-mails Sara had received to Ryan's friend at the internet café. Ryan had given one set of the e-mails to Westwood but he had another set in his office.

Guests on the morning boat asked Danny and me for details about the murders, Sara's disappearance and why Ryan was in jail. All of these events had received considerable attention in the U.S. press.

Danny and I claimed ignorance, saying only that we were absolutely certain Ryan was innocent of any wrongdoing whatsoever.

When the boat departed in the afternoon, I went into Ryan's office. Since his computer was gone I set my laptop in its place and got on the internet. Rebooking our flight wasn't easy; space on planes flying out of Bonamer was tight because tourists were leaving the island en masse. I got Danny and Weasel on an early morning flight three days later, me on one that same evening. We had driven down from Cliffview together, leaving Danny's car in the cheapest parking lot. The guys would have to wait for me at LAX.

I stuffed the Tattletail e-mails into a manila envelope. Thinking I might go grocery shopping too, I took the van keys from Ryan's desk. They were next to his cell phone. Since my cell didn't work on Bonamer, I dropped Ryan's in my purse.

Instead of passing the police station, I made an impulsive turn into its parking lot. Maybe Westwood would let me talk to Ryan. To my astonishment, I was allotted 10 minutes with him in a little room. He brightened when he saw me. We discussed the inn's business and how he would cope with our departure.

"Two people have agreed to work for me. I would appreciate it if you would call and ask if they can start right away. Not that two new employees will save my business. I need to get out of jail."

"Have they charged you with anything?" I asked.

Ryan shook his head and his face darkened. "They grilled me for hours, asking the same questions over and over. I've told them everything I know, even why we moved Van Slyke's body.

"Westwood thinks I killed Les, which is insane. I had no reason to do that. I liked Les. He and I were friends."

"Les may have been murdered with a baseball bat," I told him. "Westwood confiscated yours. When tests prove it wasn't used to kill Les, they'll have to let you go."

"I'm not holding my breath till that happens," Ryan said.

I told him I was on my way to the internet café. "I think there's a link between those e-mails and all the bad stuff that's happened. Knowing who sent them might help solve the murders.

"Oh, I hope you don't mind that I have your cell phone."

"No problem. All the local numbers are programmed into it, even the number for this station."

I said, "Don't give up hope. We'll get you out somehow."

Kenny, the proprietor of the internet café, knew who I was though I didn't remember meeting him. I showed him the e-mails and explained why they were important.

"Ryan would have brought these in but he's in jail," I said.

"So I heard. He's a friend. I'll do anything I can to get him out. But it would help if I could examine the computer they were sent to," Kenny said.

"The police took it," I said.

"That means I'll have to check my logs to see who was using our computers on the dates and times the e-mails were sent. Then I'll have to find out if the e-mails were sent from any of those computers.

"I can check the logs right now but finding out if the e-mails came from one of our computers could take awhile."

While I watched over his shoulder, Kenny pulled up the logs for the day Sara received the first e-mail. Next, he found the time.

"Four computers were in use when this was sent." He rattled off four names, only one of which I recognized.

Kenny used the same process with two other e-mails. Paul

Metsalaer was using an internet café computer when they were sent, too.

"Is Paul a regular customer?" I asked.

"Not really. He comes in when his computer is down. I don't know what he does to it but it crashes frequently. You do realize his being here doesn't mean anything unless I can trace those e-mails to the computers he was using, don't you?" Kenny cautioned.

"I understand," I said. "Still, it seems like a heck of a coincidence, doesn't it?"

As I walked to the grocery store, I mulled over what I'd just learned. Why would Paul send nasty e-mails to Sara? Was he getting back at Ryan for firing him?

Paul and Laurie had been lovers once. Had Paul tried to rekindle the romance and killed her when she rejected him? Had he killed Les? If so, why?

There was a huge roach lying on its back near the supermarket doorway. These creatures were just as repulsive dead as alive. Once again, the image of Les squashing one popped up in my mind. He'd used a wooden baseball bat.

A bat had probably been used to kill both Les and Laurie. I looked at my watch. It was just after 2:00 pm. Bonamer dive boats all went out about the same time. They wouldn't return for at least another hour. With Les dead, Paul would have to run North Shore's boat. His dive shop should be empty.

I remembered where Les had set that bat. I'd run up there and peek through the window. If it was still there, I'd call Westwood on Ryan's cell and insist he come check it out.

The drive to the little shop took about ten minutes. The only vehicles in the parking lot were a pick-up truck and a moped. I parked next to the truck, walked around to the front of the store and looked through the window. I didn't see anyone inside. Unfortunately, the corner where Les had put the bat wasn't visible. Damn.

I tried the door. It wasn't locked. Calling "Hello! Anybody here?" I went in.

It was cool and very quiet. Nobody answered my greeting. I looked around. The bat was in its place, in the corner under the whiteboard. I pulled Ryan's cell phone from my purse and scrolled down the list of contacts to the number listed for Bonamer PD. I pressed a button to dial it and turned to leave the store, bumping smack into Paul.

Chapter 39

I screamed and dropped the phone. "You scared the hell out of me," I said as I stooped to pick it up.

Paul snatched the phone from my hand and looked at the number I'd dialed.

"Why are you calling the police?" He cancelled the call and glared at me. For the first time I realized how big he was, at least 6'2."

My throat constricted and I was, for once, speechless.

"Why are you tippy-toeing around in my store and why do you think anything here would interest the police?"

My voice returned as a croak. "Ryan's in jail and I have been trying to reach him all day," I lied. "The cops keep telling me he's unavailable and I should try again later."

Paul's face showed no expression. "What are you doing here?"

I sighed, stalling for time. The next words that came out of my mouth were a surprise even to me. "A while back Ryan told us Les had something that belonged to him. I decided to look for it."

Paul snorted. "What does he think Les took?"

"A rare book. One autographed by Jacques-Yves Cousteau."

"Ryan told you that book was his? That's a lie. Les' dad bought that book for him when he was a little kid. He got Cousteau's autograph at a dive show years later."

"That's what Les told Danny and me last week. When we mentioned that to Ryan, however, he said the book was probably his. He bought one at garage sale 20 years ago. It disappeared shortly after he moved here.

"Ryan said Cousteau added a date after the signature in his book. Where is it? Let's check it out."

Paul allowed himself a tiny smile. "Les should never have left something that valuable out in the open. It's in a safe place now, where thieves can't get it."

"The book should be returned to its rightful owner," I said.

"To Ryan? I don't think so. Besides, it's his word against Les' and I believed Les when he said it was his."

Just then a man stalked into the shop. He wore rumpled khaki shorts and a navy blue t-shirt stained with grease. His face was red and streaked with sweat. He was almost as tall as Paul, with eyes that same pale blue. Paul would look like that in 25 years, when he had considerably less hair and a bigger belly.

The older Metsalaer ignored me and spoke rapidly to his son in Dutch.

When the tirade ended, Paul answered, also in Dutch, pointing to me. Then he said in English. "I don't have any more time to waste, I have a boat to fix. Get out of here. Now. And don't come back."

I mustered my dignity and strolled out of the shop. Once outside, I ran to the van and jumped inside. I started the motor and put the pedal to the metal. While I wasn't sure why, the encounter with Paul had truly disturbed me.

On the way through town I thought of stopping at the internet café and asking Kenny if he'd traced Sara's e-mails but I didn't. I wanted to get back to the SeaSide Inn, to have friends around me and feel safe once more.

I kept one eye on the van's rearview mirror, half expecting to see Paul's pick-up truck behind me. I breathed a sigh of relief when I pulled into the SeaSide Inn's driveway.

The door to the dive shop was ajar. I was sure I'd locked it when I left. I pushed it open and looked inside.

Sara stood behind the counter, her cell phone held to one ear.

Chapter 40

Sara learned her husband was the chief suspect in the deaths of Laurie and Les when she arrived at the Bonamer airport and ran into a friend.

"He's in the Bonamer jail. The police arrested him," the friend told her.

Now Sara was really worried. There was no question in her mind that Ryan was innocent. That meant a killer was running amok on Bonamer, murdering people she knew.

Sara's head reeled. Her husband needed a good lawyer, not that hack he'd hired when they were jailed after Neils' death. A quality lawyer would cost money and, unless the SeaSide Inn continued to function, there wouldn't be any coming in. Sara would have to run it alone and had no idea how to do that.

Sara's cell phone didn't work once the *California Girl* left Bonamer so she didn't turn it on until she was back in the SeaSide Inn dive shop. She called Karin first. After what Sara and Ryan had done for her, Karin owed them a huge favor.

When a robotic voice told Sara that Karin's business phone was no longer in service, Sara wasn't too concerned, she simply dialed Karin's home phone. When she found that it and Karin's cell phone number had been disconnected, Sara was beside herself. Where was Karin?

Her phone rang and she answered it without thinking.

"Do one last thing for me," Paul said. "Then I'll be out of your life forever."

Sara listened helplessly to his instructions. He had just finished talking when Cinnamon walked into the shop.

Chapter 41

Sara put her cell phone away and came out from behind the counter. We shared a brief but fierce hug.

"Welcome back," I said. "Boy, am I glad to see you. Everyone will be relieved that you're okay."

Sara said, "I missed Bonamer. I didn't think I would but I did."

"Where have you been?"

"In Aruba. I needed some time to myself."

"What did you do?"

"Not much. Went to the beach, took long walks. Mostly I just tried to figure things out. I was so confused and angry."

"Ryan told us Neils died in Karin's apartment and she asked you to help her move his body."

"Stupid me, when she called I rushed right over. I even got Ryan involved. Karin returned the favor by letting us sit in jail. Her sole concern was snagging another meal ticket to replace Neils."

"We saw the e-mails you received that claimed Ryan and Laurie were having an affair. Were those a reason you left?"

Sara seemed to consider that. "Ryan knew how hard it was for me to see Laurie every day yet he refused to fire her. The e-mails made me think there was a reason she was still around."

"Laurie loaned Ryan money to keep the inn solvent," I said. "He couldn't fire her until he paid her back. He was afraid to tell you."

Sara sighed. "It doesn't matter any more. Laurie's dead. And I finally realized Ryan couldn't possibly be having an affair with anyone. We're almost never apart and he doesn't have time."

"We're trying to trace those e-mails. They may have been sent by Paul."

"Paul Metsalaer? Why would he..." Sara began. Her face paled.

"Oh. To get back at Ryan for firing him."

"Did you know Les was dead?"

"Yes. I can't believe they suspect Ryan. He isn't a violent man. He wouldn't hurt anyone."

"Les may have been killed with a baseball bat. The police confiscated Ryan's yesterday. When the tests show it wasn't used to kill Les, I think they'll let him go. Have you been to the jail to see him?"

"I'll call right now," Sara said.

"Don't call. Just go down there and demand to see your husband. Don't leave till you do."

I handed her the van keys and, after a moment's hesitation, she left the store.

Danny's boat was at the dock, offloading divers. I told him and Weasel that Sara was back and related the reason she had given me for why she left as we prepared for the next day, when a few new guests would arrive.

We had closed the store and were headed to our apartment when Sara drove up in the van. Ryan sat in the passenger seat. When they got of the van, they clung to each other like the long-separated lovers they were.

"They decided to let him go," Sara said, teary eyed. "I got there just in time to give him a ride home."

Weasel wanted to take everyone out to dinner. It was his last night; he was going home in the morning. While Ryan and Sara declined, Danny and I were happy to take Weasel up on his offer.

Chapter 42

Ryan and Sara stepped into their yard, pulling the gate closed behind them. Danny, Weasel and I were headed to our apartment when Julie opened the door to her suite.

"We're celebrating Ryan's release from jail with dinner out. Want to join us?" Weasel said. "I'm buying."

"No thanks," she said.

"We'll be leaving in an hour or so," Weasel said. "Let us know if you change your mind."

"Will do," Julie answered.

We were all at the kitchen table, working on camera gear when Sara knocked on the door, then stuck her head in.

"FedEx just called," she said. "A package arrived for you from the States, Cinnamon. They'll be closing in 15 minutes, we just have time to get there. It's a bit out of the way so I'll drive. Don't forget your ID."

"I'm not expecting anything from anybody, I wonder what it is and who it's from," I grabbed my purse and followed Sara downstairs.

Sara was not in a talkative mood. I made several attempts at conversation and gave up when she didn't respond. She wouldn't look at me and concentrated on driving.

Twenty minutes passed. I asked, "Are you sure we can get there in time?" We seemed to be in the middle of nowhere, surrounded by desert.

"The agent said he'd wait for us."

Ten minutes later she pulled into a dirt parking lot in front of an old, rundown warehouse with a rusty tin roof. There were no other cars and the place looked deserted.

"Are you sure this is the…"

"Don't mind the appearance," Sara said. "FedEx is moving to a newer facility next week. They've already taken their signs down."

She opened the door of the building and I stepped inside.

The place was empty. Light filtered through filthy windows and the floor was covered with dust.

Dread overcame me. And then there was nothing.

Chapter 43

I regained consciousness as Paul dropped my head and shoulders on the floor in the back of the SeaSide Inn van. He frowned when he noticed I was awake. Sara carried my feet. When our eyes met she quickly looked away, her face pale and strained.

My head ached. There was a gag in my mouth, my hands were tied behind my back and my ankles were bound. I wiggled onto my side and watched as they loaded Paul's moped into the van beside me.

What on earth was going on? They must think I knew something I didn't. Or else I knew something I didn't know I knew.

Paul and Sara got into the van. Paul drove.

"I don't like this. You said you only wanted to talk to her," Sara said.

"I do want to talk to her. In a nice quiet place where we won't be interrupted."

"Take me home first. I won't say anything to anybody."

"I know you won't tell anyone. If you do you'll be locked up in one of those tiny cells for the rest of your life."

"I haven't done anything," Sara protested.

"Oh, but you have. You brought Cinnamon to me. You're going to be an accessory to murder."

"You're going to kill her? Why?" Sara's voice cracked.

"She's been snooping around. Looking for the Cousteau book. Trying to find the bat."

"What bat?"

"The less you know, the better. Just take my word for it, she knows way too much."

We drove in silence for a long time. The floor of the van was metal with a thin vinyl cover. It was more than a little uncomfortable. I tried to loosen my bonds without success. The light began to fade. It would soon be dark. At first the ride was smooth, then it became bumpy. We had gotten off the main road and onto a dirt road.

Finally the van stopped. I could hear waves pounding on the shore.

"What now?" Sara asked. She sounded weepy.

"Come with me," Paul ordered.

They got out of the van. Paul opened the back doors, which let in a welcome breeze. With Sara's help, he took the moped out.

"Get back in the van and stay there, Sara," Paul ordered.

He grabbed my feet and dragged me partway out of the van before reaching into another pocket in his shorts and bringing out a small knife, which clicked open. A shiver of fear ran through me. The knife glinted as it sliced through the line tied around my ankles.

Paul hauled me all of the way out of the van and tried to set me upright. My legs were numb and refused to function. I collapsed on the ground.

"Get up," Paul commanded.

I tried to stand but with my hands bound and my legs rubbery, I could not.

Paul used the knife to free my hands. I tugged the gag off my mouth and rubbed my arms and legs to get the circulation going.

"Stand up or I'll use this." Paul waved the small, sharp knife.

When I did manage to get upright on wobbly legs, Paul gripped my left arm and dragged me toward the sea.

The ground turned to jagged limestone, which was hard to walk on. I stumbled and started to fall. Paul hefted me onto my feet. He was very strong.

We stopped at the edge of a cliff. There was no beach below, only an angry-looking ocean lapping at the bottom of the cliff. A wave of fear washed over me.

"When I count to three, you will jump," Paul said.

Chapter 44

"Don't do this, Paul. Please," Sara said. She'd followed us.

"Get back in the van."

"You killed Laurie and Les, didn't you?" I said. "Why?"

Paul shrugged. "Why not? Laurie was going to get the *California Girl* job. That was supposed to be mine. I needed it. She didn't. She came to see Les before her appointment with the Grahams, bragging about how great it was going to be. Rubbing it in that she'd be diving the world from a luxury yacht while I was stuck here."

"Why kill Les?" I asked.

"He was a loser."

"The killing has got to stop," Sara said. I heard desperation in her voice.

Paul turned to look at her. "Who's going to stop me, Sara? You?"

Sara had distracted Paul, giving me an opportunity to act. I aimed the heel of my foot at his groin. The angle was awkward and I missed my target. While it couldn't have hurt much it did annoy Paul.

"Bitch," he said. He raised his hand to hit me just as Sara rammed the bottom of her foot into the side of his knee. She did it swiftly and forcefully and the thick, hard rubber soles of her sandals were very effective.

Paul's leg collapsed and he started to go down, grabbing Sara's arm.

I kicked him again, much harder, and my foot connected with Paul's genitals. He bellowed in pain and flung Sara over the cliff as he doubled over.

Sara screamed.

"Bitches!" Paul shouted. When he grabbed me and tried to toss me off the cliff I seized hold of his tank top and we tumbled off the precipice together.

He let go of me before we hit the ocean. I swam as far as I could, holding my breath until I couldn't stay underwater any longer. When I came up, I swiveled 360 degrees, looking for Paul and Sara. The waves were much bigger than they'd seemed from above. Their size and the fading light made it difficult to see anything.

Also worrisome, there was no beach in either direction, only miles of tall, rocky cliffs. I would not be climbing out of the sea any time soon.

I did another 360 degree reconnaissance. Where was Paul? The last gleams of sunlight danced upon the waves, playing tricks on my mind. Then I did see a glimmer of blond hair in the dying light and arms slicing rhythmically through the water. Paul, much bigger and stronger than Sara or me, was swimming against the current.

"Stupid bitches. Happy shark feeding," he yelled, his words carried to me on the wind. Then he was gone.

A few minutes later I spotted another head, a dark one, bobbing in the water. Sara wasn't far away.

"I'm sorry, sorry, sorry," she said when I reached her. "I didn't know..."

I interrupted. "Where are we?"

Sara was well aware of my navigational limitations. "On the east side. The current is taking us north."

I looked at the shore. No lights were blinking on as the twilight deepened.

"No one lives here?"

"No. Nobody comes here after dark either."

"Any places to get out of the water?"

"Not till we get to the north end. If we get there."

"Why is Paul swimming the other way?"

"He's headed toward Lac Bay."

"Shouldn't we go that way, too?"

"No. The current is too strong and Lac Bay is too far away. Paul won't make it, he only thinks he will."

"The beaches at the north end are in the national park, right? What happens if we miss them?"

"We'll get swept out to sea and die."

"Okay. We'll stay close to shore so we can get out at the first beach. How long will that take?"

"Hours. These waters are full of sharks, Cinnamon. We'll never make it."

"Look, Sara. You got me into this and you are going to help me get out. Don't waste energy whining."

We drifted in silence for a while. The water, warm when you're wearing a wetsuit, was chilly without one. When we tried to conserve body heat by hugging our knees with our arms, swells hit us in the face and Sara whimpered. I worried we wouldn't see the beach when we got to it. We needed to stay awake and alert.

"Were you having an affair with Paul?" I asked, hoping to take Sara's mind off her misery.

"Yes."

"Why?"

"To pay Ryan back for sleeping with Laurie."

"We know about the e-mails you were getting about that. Didn't you wonder who sent them?"

"Of course. I thought it might be Laurie. It never occurred to me it was Paul. He initiated our affair. I'd never really liked him all that much but he's younger than I am and I was flattered by his attention. At first I just wanted Ryan to find out and be sorry. He was totally oblivious. An entire month and he never suspected a thing."

"Did you know Paul was going to kill Laurie?"

"Oh God no. That was a total shock. Everybody but me liked her."

"Why did you really go to Aruba?"

"Les had a copy of the Jacques Cousteau book, *The Silent World*. He said it was nearly priceless because it was a first edition and contained Cousteau's signature."

I said, "I saw the book in the North Shore Diving shop. It was gone when I went there after Les died."

"That's because Paul decided to finance his escape from Bonamer by selling it. He ordered another copy online and switched the two books. I think Les found out so Paul killed him.

"In Paul's mind he was the perfect person for the *California Girl* job. He knew the boat was headed to Aruba when it left here and had already contacted a dealer there about selling the book. Once he had the money from the sale, he'd tell the Grahams he'd changed his mind about working for them and would be free to do whatever he wanted for the rest of his life."

"But the Grahams didn't hire him," I said. "So he had no way to get to Aruba."

"Right. He knew they'd take me, though, which they did.

"When the book sold, the money would be deposited electronically in Paul's bank account. He said he would meet me in Aruba and give me a generous fee for helping him sell it."

"The book was worthless, wasn't it?"

"How did you know?"

"If the book was really valuable, Les would have sold it and used the money to keep his dive operation open."

"I didn't think of that."

"Did you really believe Paul would keep his word?"

Sara shrugged. "Sure."

"He'd already killed two people, Sara."

"I didn't know that then. I've been such an idiot."

I agreed but kept my mouth shut. We didn't talk for quite some time. As the evening wore on, the wind quieted and the water got calmer. I kept my eyes trained on the shoreline, hoping Sara was wrong and we'd be able to get out of the ocean sooner than she expected.

"Ryan told me your dad raised you," Sara said without preamble. "Was it hard growing up without a mother?"

I thought about that for a little bit. "My mom was only around full time until I was two or three, when she began traveling with her band. I spent a lot of time at the camera store with my Dad. He and his staff gave me a lot of attention.

"My parents divorced when I was five. Mom died when I was eight. She hadn't been a big part of my life for years by then and I didn't miss her very much."

"Was your Dad bitter about her leaving?"

"If he was I never saw it. They were married six years, together full time only three. He told me once that he always knew she wouldn't be around forever. He said her heart was set on being a star and that wasn't ever going to happen in Cliffview."

"Wasn't puberty difficult without a mom? My pop would die a thousand deaths if he had to discuss female plumbing with me or help me shop for a bra."

I laughed. "Dad was very happy to leave those things to my best friend's mother, who treated me like a second daughter."

"Where did your parents meet?"

"At a party in college. She was a freshman, he was a senior. He said it was like lightning struck him, he fell in love with her instantly. They were married six months later. When I was a teenager I asked him if they got married because she was pregnant with me. He stammered, turned red and admitted they did. That was a shameful thing in those days."

There was a brief silence, then Sara said, "Ryan says Danny wants to get married. He told Danny if you really loved him you wouldn't keep turning him down."

That made me bristle. "Ryan should mind his own business. True, I'm not eager to get married again, I only just got divorced. But I do love Danny. It will happen eventually."

"How about kids? Ryan let me know he didn't want them on our first date. That was okay with me. I don't think I'm cut out for motherhood."

"That could be a problem," I admitted. "Danny wants at least one more, he thinks two would be even better. I don't know if I want any."

"Maybe that's because your mom deserted you. Maybe you're afraid you won't be a good mother."

That was a sucker punch. I'd never admitted that to myself, not ever. I wasn't going to think about it now.

We were in the ocean a long, long time. We were tired and cold and conversation took too much effort. The night got very dark, lit only by a crescent moon and a million stars. We tried to stay warm by putting our arms around each other and floating along that way.

We had hallucinations. I saw a ship all lit up and urged Sara to swim toward it, sure of our rescue. It was a mirage, and when it vaporized, we were far from shore. Sara didn't say anything but I heard her weeping.

The swim back to the coastline was exhausting.

Several times I thought something brushed up against my legs. Sara felt things too. We were afraid to look into the inky depths but when we did, there was nothing there. In the beginning we were terrified sharks would rip us to shreds. Near the end, we were so miserable we would have welcomed that.

We were shivering uncontrollably by the time we saw a white sandy beach gleaming in the moonlight. Hope filled my heart. Then I wondered if it was just another mirage.

No matter. We had to go for it before the current carted us past it. We headed in. It took all the energy we had. We didn't stop to time the swells and go in when there was a lull, we just kicked toward shore with the last of our ebbing strength.

A wave crashed over us in the surf line. I lost sight of Sara as I was sucked down into a washing machine-like maelstrom. Just when I thought I couldn't hold my breath any longer and would surely drown, I was deposited on shore. Waves washed over me and I dug my hands into the sand. Each time the water receded, I crawled forward. Four times the ocean sent heavy, frothy arms to reclaim me, but it failed and I was finally beyond its reach on dry land.

I inched up the slope, reveling in the warmth of the air and the sand. I rolled over and over until a thick coat of sand covered all but my face. Then I closed my eyes and went to sleep.

Chapter 45

I awoke disoriented. It was still dark. My lips were cracked and parched, my flesh soft and prune-like from so many hours in the sea. I was horribly thirsty.

I looked for Sara, half expecting to find her dead in the surf line. Instead, she lay on the beach about ten feet away.

I crawled over to her, not sure if she was alive.

"Wake up, Sara. We have to go. When the sun comes up we'll fry."

There was no response. I shook her.

"So tired."

I tried to rouse her again and again. Finally I said, "If you stay here, Paul will find you."

Her eyes fluttered open then and we were soon on our way. Sara was the walking dead. It took all she had to remain upright and move forward. I couldn't help her. I, too, was drained.

A vague picture of the park, from Danny's and my visit, formed in my brain. The park entrance couldn't be far. I found the beginning of a road and we followed it to a fork.

"Which way?"

Sara looked around slowly, then lurched straight ahead. I followed.

I had sand everywhere. It dried as I walked and I shook if off my clothes. The sand in my sandals was painful. I sat down, took them off and carefully brushed it off.

We had to pick our way carefully in the moonlight. The road was unpaved, full of potholes and rocks.

I had to look out for Sara. I was afraid if she fell, she'd never get back up.

Then I noticed the cactus.

Dad and I had camped in California deserts several times. He insisted I learn survival techniques, which included cutting open a cactus and sucking on the pulp to get moisture. In California we'd used a large, fixed-blade hunting knife. Here, I took the longest sharp rock I found and went to work on a prickly pear. It was much harder than I expected. I almost gave up half a dozen times. I scraped off the spines, a few of which found their way into my palms and fingers. I sliced into the cactus.

The pulp was air temperature-warm and bitter. I had to chew it to get what little moisture it offered.

Sara spit out the first piece I gave her. I forced another on her and we stumbled onward.

I was in the lead when we came to a four-way intersection. Green flags pointed one direction; yellow and green flags pointed another. The road we stood on and a fourth road had no flags. "Shit." I sank to the ground. If I had the energy and my dehydrated body could make tears, I would have cried.

"What?" Sara asked.

"I don't know which way to go."

Sara looked at the plethora of flags. "No flags. That way." She tried to point but that required too much effort. She teetered down an unmarked road.

We walked and walked and walked. Occasionally, we stopped to rest or cut open a cactus. The dirt became pavement as the sky brightened in the east. We came to a deep dip in the road. I remembered it. When we reached the top of the far side, we would see the park entrance.

The wrought iron gate entrance to the park was closed and locked. On both sides of it a fence of barbed wire and live cactus stretched as far as we could see.

I felt as if I were moving in slow motion. It had taken forever to get here. My last thought as I slid to the ground with my back against the gate was that rangers would find us when the park opened. We had reached the end of our long and arduous journey.

I was in and out of consciousness after that. I heard someone say, "It's them all right. I saw their pictures on TV last night."

The hard ground gave way to something soft. Voices spoke in whispers. I was way too tired to open my eyes.

Chapter 46

Julie had come to Bonamer after learning Cinnamon would be there from the society column in the Cliffview Chronicle. She thought it would be easier to get to know Cinnamon when she was on vacation, plus the island was a neutral locale where neither of them had any history.

Yet instead of the relaxed, carefree atmosphere she'd expected, Julie had dropped into a hornet's nest. Before she arrived there'd been the mysterious death of a golf course developer. Worse, two more dead bodies were found not long after she set foot on Bonamer.

Julie lived in Oakland, California, which had a notoriously high crime rate. There, these events would have been small ripples on a stormy sea. Here, on this tranquil island, they had the impact of a tsunami.

Getting to Bonamer had been less difficult than she'd expected. News of the Neils Van Slyke's "murder" roared across the internet like a major fire, resulting in a flurry of flight and resort cancellations. Airfares plummeted. By the time the "murder" was revealed as a natural death and bookings began to rebound, Julie had her plane tickets and a room at the GrapeTree, right next door to the SeaSide Inn. After Laurie and Les were killed and so many SeaSide guests left early, the inn had plenty of vacancies and she was able to move there. Being so close to Cinnamon was both exciting and anxiety provoking.

Getting to the point where she was ready to re-establish a relationship with Cinnamon had taken years. Julie couldn't think about that without remembering how it all began.

Jimmy Greene, who couldn't take his eyes off her from the get-go, was the nicest boy Julie had ever met: smart, kind, sincere and considerate. Everybody liked him. While not movie star handsome, he had curly red hair, green eyes, an infectious smile and a slender build. His face lit up when he looked at Julie. That was pretty heady stuff and for several months she thought she loved him.

She found out she was pregnant not long after the initial glow of the relationship began to wear off. She liked Jimmy a lot; he was a wonderful friend. But she didn't love him, not the way he loved her. She married him anyway. In those days abortions weren't legal and even if they were, her religion forbade them and she knew her parents would never consent to putting their only grandchild up for adoption.

In the beginning, Julie thought the marriage might work. Jimmy was four years older than she was and got a job in Cliffview when he graduated. Julie was excited about moving to California and her new husband was intent upon making her happy.

Then the baby came. Julie was only 19. Suddenly she had no life. Every hour was devoted to the care of an infant who had colic and would cry for hours on end no matter what Julie did. Jimmy helped as much as he could but he had a full-time job.

Julie loved the baby, though she felt like a failure when she couldn't get her to stop crying. Worse, she began to resent not being able to do all the things her former college classmates were doing. While they were enjoying parties and dates, she was stuck at home, engaged in a never-ending, energy-sapping cycle of diaper changing, feeding, laundry, cooking and house cleaning. She and Jimmy had moved to Cliffview only a few months before the baby was born and Julie had no friends there, nobody at all besides Jimmy to talk to.

After the first couple years, Julie's child rearing chores became a little more tolerable. Still, deep down inside she knew it was only a matter of time before she left Jimmy. While he had all the qualities women say they want in a man, he wasn't a rock star and never would be. And, always having had love and security, Julie did not appreciate their value.

Her first step to freedom was singing with a local band at Flanagan's, Cliffview's most popular bar, on the weekends. That made Julie more than just a wife and mother, it made her a person with a job and contacts outside the family circle. Jake was the lead singer of the band and she quickly fell in love with him. Nothing came of that for a while because he already had a girlfriend. Jake and Julie, however, had a common bond. They had aspirations that stretched way beyond a small town on the California coast.

Jimmy was not happy when the band got a gig at a club on the Sunset Strip and Julie began spending several nights a week in Hollywood. When Jake broke up with his girlfriend, he and Julie hooked up. Though she didn't tell Jimmy, somehow he knew.

The band got a long-term gig in San Francisco and Julie didn't come home at all for several months. When she did, it was to ask for a divorce.

All Jimmy wanted was full custody of Cinnamon, which was fine with Julie. She thought Jake would marry her when her divorce was final but he didn't. He also insisted she stop making even infrequent visits to Cliffview to see Cinnamon, claiming they kept her from focusing all her attention on the band.

Drugs were always around. Julie resisted them for a while, then began taking them just to fit in. Later, they helped drown the guilt she felt for deserting her child and husband. Jake made sure there were always plenty on hand.

Everyone believed the band was on the brink of making it big when they moved to San Francisco. Though there was a lot of interest in their demo record, nothing ever came of it. Jake blamed Julie, saying her voice wasn't unique and she lacked stage presence. He hired a new female lead and Julie was out. Things went downhill rapidly after that and the band broke up.

Julie became a homeless addict with no job and no skills. She did what she had to do to survive in the next couple of decades. She also went through rehab four times.

On several occasions during those clean and sober periods, Julie borrowed a car and visited Cliffview, where she watched her ex-husband and child as they went about their daily activities. They never noticed her because years earlier, while she listened in a drug induced haze, Jake had called her parents and told them their only child had died in a car accident and her body had been cremated. He sent them a box of ashes he'd collected from the fireplace, claiming they were Julie's.

A fire destroyed Julie's childhood home, killing her parents, before she corrected the lie. The guilt was overwhelming. Sober, Julie couldn't face what she'd done. Over the years, however, she got tired of being a loser. There was still time to do something worthwhile with her life.

She had gone through her last rehab three years ago. She was pretty sure this one had taken. While it was too late to make amends to her parents, there was still time to set things right with her daughter.

Once she arrived on Bonamer, Julie was eager to meet Cinnamon. She walked over to the SeaSide Inn right after she checked in at the GrapeTree. That was the day Laurie's body was found and the place was deserted. She came by again later but the shop was still closed and Cinnamon and crew nowhere to be seen.

The next day, when she entered the shop to ask about renting a room, Cinnamon was behind the counter. Julie hadn't been this close to her for more than two decades. She tried not to, but she couldn't help staring. Although their coloring was different, the mother/daughter resemblance was striking. Looking at Cinnamon, Julie saw a younger, redheaded version of herself. It made her want to cry tears of regret.

Later that day, Julie watched Cinnamon, Danny and Weasel head into town. She figured they were going out to dinner and followed them. They were so intent on their conversation that they didn't notice her tagging along behind them. She was elated when they invited her to sit at their table. Unfortunately, they were much more curious than she expected. Julie wasn't prepared to answer all those questions just yet. She didn't want to lie, either, so she remained vague. She was sure they thought her more than a little strange.

After Les' body was discovered, Julie found the invitation to spend the night in Cinnamon's apartment too wonderful to turn down. It had been eventful. Cinnamon's quest to kill the cockroach would have been funny if Ryan hadn't appeared, armed with a bat. Someone could have gotten hurt. After that, even Julie, an Oakland-toughened former street person, began to feel a bit uneasy.

When they gathered on the balcony to have coffee the next morning, all of those eyes scrutinizing her and Cinnamon really rattled Julie. She wasn't ready to tell Cinnamon why they looked so much alike. Alone in her room later, Julie took a deep breath and willed herself to relax. She was trembling.

She would have liked going out on the boat with them that day but didn't think she should subject herself to any more questions, especially from her daughter, who seemed to have inherited a gene from someone that made her disconcertingly curious and direct.

Now Julie's plans had gone completely awry. Cinnamon was missing and Julie might never have a chance to make up for those lost years.

That was really, really difficult. Two of the people she'd hurt were beyond her reach. She would never be able to tell them how sorry she was for all the pain she had caused. The regret and guilt she felt about that were the reasons she had failed to stay sober in the past. Now her daughter might be lost to her forever.

Julie needed a drink.

Chapter 47

Danny's worried face was the first thing I saw when I awakened in Bonamer's tiny hospital. He looked tired and disheveled. When he noticed my eyes were open, he bent to kiss my cheek. "How do you feel?"

"Alive. How's Sara?"

"She'll survive. What the heck happened? We looked for you everywhere."

"It's a long story. Could I have something to eat first? I'm starving."

Danny left the room and returned a few minutes later with a tray of food. As I ate, he related what had transpired after Sara and I left, supposedly for the FedEx office.

"When you weren't back after 40 minutes, I went to see Ryan. Sara had told him she needed something from the drugstore, which closed shortly after she left. He hadn't realized how long she'd been gone till I showed up.

"We took Sara's car to FedEx, which is only five minutes from the inn. It had been closed for more than hour. We drove through the town, looking for the van.

"We didn't know what to think. We went to the police station. Westwood said you hadn't been gone long enough to be considered missing.

"I had a bad feeling. Ryan did, too. He enlisted the help of No Tees members and pretty soon a couple hundred people were looking for the van.

"The island has a lot of little dirt roads. Someone finally came across the van and Paul's moped early this morning."

"Did you find Paul?"

"Not so far."

Danny noticed I'd finished eating. "Now, will you tell me what happened?"

So I did. When Weasel arrived, I told him, too. Westwood showed up in the middle of that account and I started over. When I finally finished, Westwood left, saying he'd send deputies to look for Paul along the coast.

I was released from the hospital late that afternoon. It's amazing I got any rest while I was there. I had a steady stream of visitors: Danny, Weasel, Ryan, Westwood and, much to my surprise, Julie.

"I was so worried about you," she said. "Thank goodness you're okay. I am so thankful you made it through alive.

"When you're up to it I'd like to talk to you," she added.

I was about to say, "How about now?" when Westwood entered the room. It was time for one of the extensive interviews about our ordeal that he had been conducting with Sara and me.

"See you later," Julie said and slipped from the room.

I never saw her on Bonamer again. Danny said she checked out of the SeaSide Inn just before I left the hospital.

Danny, Weasel and I flew home the next day. Westwood was at the airport to usher us through check-in and security. Danny wasn't fooled by the VIP treatment. "That man really wants you off his island," he remarked.

No matter what Westwood thinks, none of what happened on Bonamer was my fault.

Though there'd been no sign of Paul, Sara and I were convinced he'd survived his swim and was hiding somewhere. Since she wasn't leaving the island like I was, that made Sara anxious.

All of the Millers' secrets were out in the open at long last. After we got home, Sara e-mailed me that they had agreed to forget the past and start over. I thought they really loved each other and hoped their union would prosper.

I was glad to be home in California and out of Paul's reach. I considered it a miracle Sara and I had survived our encounter with him.

I guess that Danny and Weasel felt the same way. They were annoyingly solicitous. Luckily, that treatment was short-lived. And finally alone in my condo, I relished the peace and quiet.

Life was quickly back to normal. Dad was happy I'd gotten home in one piece. After all, I was his favorite (not to mention only) daughter. His wife (my stepmother, Sandy) could hardly wait to show me all the things my baby brother had learned to do while I was gone. The kid is incredibly cute and amazingly smart.

At Cliffview PD, Tony welcomed me with a smile. Chief Lawson scowled.

What remained of Paul was found a week after we left, not far from where he'd gone into the ocean. Sharks had feasted on his body and only his skull, a few bones and scraps of clothing washed ashore. Did sharks kill him? Maybe, maybe not, there wasn't enough left of him to determine that. Dental records were needed to confirm that the skull was his.

I slept exceptionally well the night I learned he was gone forever. Sara e-mailed me that she did, too.

Chapter 48

The Bonamer adventures were several weeks in the past when Dad summoned me to his office at Greene's One Stop Camera and Photo. When I opened the door and stepped inside, Julie Wade was looking at a pile of photo prints and saying, "Oh my. What a cutie. He looks so much like you, Jimmy."

That momentarily confused me. Everyone in town calls my Dad "Red," even though his hair isn't red anymore.

Dad beamed.

"Julie. What are you doing here?" I asked.

"Have a seat, Cinnamon," Dad said. "We have something to tell you."

A look I could not decipher passed between Dad and Julie. Then she said, "This isn't going to be easy." She took a deep breath. "Remember when people in Bonamer asked if we were related? Well, we are."

"Cousins? On my mother's side or Dad's?"

"We're a lot closer than that."

"Are we sisters?" I threw Dad an incredulous look. Was this a daughter he'd never told me about?

"We're not sisters, Cinnamon. Take a closer look."

I stared at her. I didn't want to see the resemblance to the woman in the photo I had kept in my bedroom for nearly three decades. How had I not noticed that sooner?

But it couldn't be. The woman in that photo died years ago.

It was hard to breathe. "My mother is dead."

"We were told she died," Dad said gently. "She didn't. She's been living in Northern California all these years."

"I don't believe that. How can you be sure it's her, Dad? You haven't seen her for 25 years."

"I knew who she was the moment she walked into the store. Believe me, it was quite a shock."

"You can't be sure," I insisted stubbornly.

"Yes, I can. There is absolutely no doubt in my mind," Dad said. "This is your mother, Cinnamon. Tell me you can't see that."

I couldn't do that. I couldn't do anything. My entire body, including my brain, was suddenly numb.

The silence wasn't a comfortable one. Julie said, "I'm sorry. This isn't the way I wanted to tell you."

"Why did you want us to think you were dead?"

"It wasn't my idea."

"Let her tell you what happened," Dad urged.

"I wasn't the only one she deserted, she deserted you, too," I blurted out.

"I came to terms with that long ago," Dad said. "Julie was only 19 when you were born. It wasn't something we planned.

"Think of yourself when you were graduating from college, Cinnamon. Would you have been happy stuck in Cliffview with a baby? You had stars in your eyes then, just like your mother did. You were going to Hollywood with your photographer husband. You knew it was only a matter of time before he'd be shooting covers for The Rolling Stone. Fame was just around the corner.

"Julie dreamed of being a singer in a rock band. Her leaving was painful but I got over it. It was a long time ago. I've had a good life. *You've* had a good life."

"You are a wonderful father. I have never wanted for anything. But it would have been nice to have a mother."

"I can't change the past," Julie said. "All I can do is try to do better in the future.

"Talk," I said. "I'm listening."

And so she did, finishing with, "Two years ago I married Lee, a man I met in rehab. We are both doing well."

"Why didn't you tell us you were alive sooner?" I asked.

"I wanted to be clean and sober. I had to be sure I wouldn't have another relapse. I had already failed three times. I almost fell off the wagon when you went missing in Bonamer and I thought you were lost forever."

She looked at me. "I visited Cliffview twice in the last year, trying to work up the courage to talk to you. I sat in my car and watched the store. I subscribed to the local paper, so I could follow what you were doing. I knew when you left Ted and returned to Cliffview. Once I even had dinner at Juanita's when you, Danny and Weasel were there.

"I was the fly on the wall. You didn't know I existed and didn't notice me."

Julie continued. "You and your Dad both looked so happy. He had a beautiful new wife, then a baby. You had a wonderful boyfriend and seemed to be enjoying life. I began to hope you'd be able to forgive me.

"Lee and my sponsor have been urging me to make my peace with both of you. It was hard to walk in here. I was surprised and grateful that Jimmy recognized me right away. He has treated me like an old friend. I can't tell you how much that means to me.

"I went to Bonamer, hoping to get to know you before I told you who I was. My plan was derailed by all the chaos."

"What do you want from me?"

"I want to be part of your life again."

"I think you gave up that right a long time ago," I said.

Chapter 49

I was extremely angry for a while. That Julie had been living just a few hours away from us for decades and had not contacted us ate away at my insides. That Dad was delighted she was alive and that he and his wife, Sandy, invited Julie and her husband to our Thanksgiving dinner, well, I thought that was wrong. How could they do that to me?

Dad, Sandy, Danny and Weasel all tried to change my mind with versions of, "So many years have been lost, life is too short to lose any more."

Danny finally got through to me. Seemingly out of the blue one night, when we were lying in bed in the dark after a particularly satisfying love making session he said: "You've been motherless for a long time but you don't have to be any more, Cinnamon. It's your choice. You can go on punishing Julie or you can let go of the past and make the best of the future."

Danny's little speech was too pat, it made me suspicious. "Did you think that up all by yourself?"

Danny chuckled. "I told Sandy you'd never believe those were my words," he admitted. "She said if it improved your disposition even a little she didn't care. We all want to enjoy Thanksgiving and you've been one hell of a wet blanket recently."

"Sandy called me a wet blanket?"

"No, I did."

"I have good reason to be angry with my mother."

"No one disputes that. But it's time to let it go, Cinnamon. You're making all of us miserable, yourself most of all. Julie made huge mistakes and paid a huge price for them. Give her a chance to show she can have a positive impact on your life."

"Sandy come up with that one?"

"No. That was Weasel and me."

"How many people were in on this?"

"Only the three of us. Red knew you'd know and wanted no part of it."

The mention of Dad brought to mind a photo he had taken of my mom. It had always sat — indeed, still sat — on a dresser in my bedroom. I didn't need to look at it, the details were burned into my memory.

It showed a very young Julie in faded jeans and a pale blue blouse. She stood hip deep in a field of golden grasses. Her hair was long, straight and the color of wheat. Strands of it blew across her face and freckled nose and one slender hand reached up to push them back. She smiled shyly at the camera.

Dad had always said the Mona Lisa smile was proof she was pregnant with me.

I loved that photo. Now I realized I had never stopped loving the woman in it.

My friends and family were right. Too many years had been lost.

"I suppose it wouldn't hurt to try," I said.

"Hooray," Danny said, relief evident in his voice.

The relationship grew through e-mails. At first there were short, tentative ones from me, answered by longer, eager ones from Julie. I began looking forward to at least one daily message and when I didn't get one, I was disappointed.

I spent a weekend in Oakland, seeing where Julie lived and worked and how she and her husband had become valued members of their community. We both noticed how alike we were. We hated peas, used the same toothpaste, loved dangly earrings and the color blue and wore the same size clothes. Our hair parted naturally on the same side. Our eyes were the same color and our faces, the same shape. Sun made our noses freckle.

Thanksgiving was huge success. Sandy's parents, brother and bachelor uncle came, along with Julie, her husband, Weasel, Danny and me.

It was mind boggling to see my parents together, each with his/her current spouse. Julie joined the adoring crowd that surrounded my baby brother, guaranteeing her instant familial acceptance. (He is a happy, giggly baby who charms everyone who lays eyes on him.) Dad and Lee, Julie's husband, were more reserved but I think a friendship will thrive there.

That dinner was so successful we're planning to celebrate Christmas as one big, happy California extended family.

Epilogue

In a surprising turn of events, the tragic events of our visit ended up boosting the SeaSide Inn's business. Because his guests kept pestering him for information on the "The Bonamer Murders," and his inn was inundated with people stopping to see where Les' body had been found, Ryan created The Murder Tours (TMT). He set up a website, painted the SeaSide Inn's van bright red and began offering tours, complete with a box lunch and a driver/guide, usually Sara. The tours proved especially popular with cruise ship visitors so Ryan bought three used school buses to accommodate them. The buses were painted the same red as the van. Four new driver/guides were hired and Sara wrote a script for them.

According to the website, the tours take visitors to certain key sites on the island, where the guide provides an account of people being killed and/or falling off a cliff into the sea.

The final stop is the Bonamer cemetery. Laurie isn't buried there, her body was cremated and her ashes scattered at sea. She is remembered, however, with a small memorial. It and the surrounding area are always covered with multitudes of colorful plastic flowers (real ones are hard to come by on Bonamer) and candles, along with a variety of plush and plastic sea creatures. Les' body was also cremated and the ashes scattered at sea. Neils' wife flew his body back to Amsterdam, where it reposes in the family mausoleum.

Sara sent me a copy of her script, which was very well written. I found her version of Paul's demise especially graphic and chilling. I don't believe I'll ever tire of reading it.

One of the people who took a murder tour turned out to be a literary agent. She sold a book based on Sara's script to a New York publisher. These days Sara isn't guiding tours, working in the dive shop or leading dives; she's hard at work on the book, which will include some of my crime scene photos. The script has been optioned as well and may become a made-for-TV movie (or not, Sara knows many more scripts are optioned than end up being used).

Ryan's newest moneymaker is a small souvenir stand he built in the inn's parking lot. The bestsellers are T-shirts with The Murder Tours map on the back, along with earrings and a keychain featuring miniature bright red TMT buses.

Ryan and Sara have granted Danny, Weasel and me lifetime visitation rights. We are welcome at the SeaSide Inn anytime for as long as we wish to stay. We expect to spend a couple of weeks there this fall. Ryan claims that when he told Westwood we planned to return to the island, he looked ill.

Acknowledgments

Many of you will recognize certain features of the fictional island of Bonamer as similar to those of Bonaire, where I have spent a great deal of time vacationing with friends and housesitting.

When I wrote this book, Bonaire was a small, sleepy island and little had changed during the 20-year span I visited it. Recently, however, the island began making giant strides into the 21st Century. The Bonaire of today bears little resemblance to the Bonaire of the past. I have borrowed from the past, the present and perhaps the future but made up people, events and anything else I needed to tell the story I wanted you to read. So while some of Bonaire's physical features may still be the same, *Murder Dives the Caribbean* is a work of fiction.

For many years I worked alone, not discussing this or any other work in progress with anyone. That changed two years ago, when I realized I needed feedback. I approached several people and most of them agreed to read my books and tell me what they thought of them. Many thanks to my wonderful readers: Janet Davies, Lynn Davies, Dave Finnern, Michele Hall, Judy Hemenway and Paul Mila. Because of them, this is a better book.

About the Author

Bonnie J. Cardone grew up in Arizona, Chicago and Michigan. She moved to Southern California in 1967 and became a scuba diver in 1973. From then on, her goal was to dive as much of the world as possible.

In 1976 she was hired as an editor of the world's largest and oldest diving magazine, Skin Diver. The next 22 years were exciting and educational. The magazine and the sport grew far larger far faster than anyone had expected. Meanwhile, Bonnie was becoming a photographer and writing hundreds of articles on almost every imaginable marine related subject.

When Bonnie was downsized in 1999, she did what she had always planned to do when she retired: she started writing mystery novels. She had already taken five UCLA extension writing classes and written several short mystery stories. At friend Gary Brandner's suggestion, she had joined Mystery Writers of America while she was a stay at home mom in the 1970s.

Bonnie joined Sisters in Crime in 1999 and, in 2000, became the editor of its national newsletter, a job that lasted nine years and provided a first class education in all aspects of the mystery field. During those years Bonnie attended two to three mystery conventions annually, meeting and photographing famous and not so famous mystery writers. She also attended author panels and interviews (and conducted a few of the latter herself for the newsletter).

At present, Bonnie is a freelancer who writes marine related articles for scuba diving publications and illustrates them with her photographs as well as writing mystery novels and short stories.

www.ingramcontent.com/pod-product-compliance
Lightning Source LLC
Chambersburg PA
CBHW030246130626
46549CB00002B/411